The Strange September
of Levi Pepperfield

The Strange September of Levi Pepperfield

For May

A Novel

Jan 25, 2019

Matthew Manera

Matthew Manera

N₁O₂N₁
CANADA

Copyright © 2019 by Matthew Manera

All rights reserved. No part of this book may be used or reproduced in any manner whatsoever without the prior written permission of the publisher, except in the case of brief quotations embodied in reviews.

Publisher's note: This book is a work of fiction. Names, characters, places and incidents are either the product of the author's imagination or are used fictitiously, and any resemblance to actual persons living or dead is entirely coincidental.

Library and Archives Canada Cataloguing in Publication

Title: The strange September of Levi Pepperfield : a novel / Matthew Manera.

Names: Manera, Matthew, 1949- author.

Identifiers: Canadiana 20190050551 | ISBN 9781988098739 (softcover)

Classification: LCC PS8626.A555 S77 2019 | DDC C813/.6—dc23

Printed and bound in Canada on 100% recycled paper.

Now Or Never Publishing
901, 163 Street
Surrey, British Columbia
Canada V4A 9T8

nonpublishing.com
Fighting Words.

We gratefully acknowledge the support of the Canada Council for the Arts and the British Columbia Arts Council for our publishing program.

for little Ernie, who knew

Yet nothing corrupts so much as *this*:
to approach people as instructor.
—Rainer Maria Rilke

. . . for the leaves were full of children,
Hidden excitedly, containing laughter.
Go, go, go, said the bird: human kind
Cannot bear very much reality,
Time past and time future
What might have been and what has been
Point to one end, which is always present.
—T.S. Eliot

Part One

My words itch at your ears till you understand them.
—Walt Whitman

"I Fart And my shit smells."

"Seriously, that's your opening line?"

"I thought we should get the difficult, yet unavoidable aspects of the human predicament out of the way first. Clear the air, as it were."

"Is that supposed to be funny?"

"No, I just wanted . . ."

"Has this line ever worked on anyone before?"

"I've never tried it before. I'm turning over a new leaf."

"Try a different leaf."

She proceeded to ignore me until the five-minute bell rang and I had to move to the next table and the next woman. Five minutes is a long time when time is all there is.

"Hi. I fart and my shit smells."

I was putting all my eggs in this one basket because I had very deliberately decided to leave all my other baskets at home. To be truthful, I had made a bonfire out of all my other baskets. I had decided to let go of every convention that had been stifling, crushing, destroying my life ever since I could remember. Which is why I was wearing mismatched argyle socks—they may not have left the sock factory together, but they were clean; Levis Relaxed Fit jeans that were one size too big—I didn't have an ass worth advertising anymore; a twenty-year-old T-shirt from a Bob Dylan concert—it might have been thirty years old, but I stopped counting these kinds of years many years (I can't remember how many) ago; a corduroy sports jacket with elbow patches—I didn't give a shit what the latest attitude to corduroy was or where on your body it was supposed to appear, if at all; a Boston Red Sox baseball cap; and a paisley silk scarf.

"You dress like a mentally deranged homeless person," the woman at table number two observed, then proceeded to manifest her silent disgust for me in the same way the first woman did. Time and more time. On to table number three.

"Hi. I fart and . . ."

"And your . . . well, it smells. Yes, I know. I overheard you from the other table."

Even in a crowded room gravelled with the uneven stones of too many voices speaking at once, unexpected words will rise like minor explosions of shape and colour out of the common verbiage, and anyone who is already momentarily distracted will perk their ears to the sound.

"Do you think you might fart in the next five minutes?" she asked.

"Probably not. If this were ten minutes long, I couldn't really make any promises. I like what you're wearing."

She had on one of those long sweater tops that hang down below the waist. Her jeans fit her better than mine did, and she wore calf-length leather boots with three-inch heels. I knew about the length of the sweater and her boots because I leaned down and looked under the table.

"Drop something?" she asked.

"No."

"What you're wearing is . . . interesting," she said, once I was sitting up straight again. "You're a Bob Dylan fan?"

"Not anymore."

"Then why are you wearing that T-shirt?"

"It's comfortable and it was next on the stack of clean T-shirts when I was getting dressed this morning."

"How big is the stack?"

"About yea high," I said, holding an invisible stack of T-shirts between my hands.

"I used to like Bob Dylan, too," she said. "Then I stopped liking him. I've stopped liking all the musicians I liked when I was younger. None of them is as good as when they first started out."

"You get that? I get that. So many artists arrive at the intersection of youth, inspiration, and creativity driving souped-up hot rods, but end up driving down the road in a Dodge minivan. Can I have your phone number?"

She looked across the hall towards the main desk where the chaperones were seated, monitoring the proceedings.

"I don't think that's how it's supposed to work."

"Fine," I said. "Here's my phone number."

I took a notepad out of my jacket pocket, wrote down my phone number, tore out the page, and handed it to her.

"It's true, though," I said.

"What is?"

"I do fart. And my shit smells. I just don't want there to be any misunderstandings going forward."

‡

The night was crisp and full of tiny million-miles-away stars as I stepped out the front doors of the hall and onto the street. I knew she would never call me, but that was beside the point. The point was that I had set out to do something—to place myself unflinchingly in a world that I was allergic to—and I had done it. I felt I could do anything now. It was September, the chill of fall had arrived early this year, and for the first time since I was five years old I was not going back to school, on either side of the desk. My life was now officially my own, whether I wanted it or not. Tonight, I wanted it, mostly.

Among other things, I wanted to get the beauty of language back. After grading first-year university English essays for thirty years, which, both in their quantity and their growing and persistent illiteracy, overwhelmed any relief that may have come my way by reading upper-level papers, I had begun to lose sense of what a grammatically correct and stylistically erotic sentence looked like. I had read so many scatologically stained sentences that I was on the verge of no longer being able to recognize the beauty of the language that was so dear to me, so necessary to me. As I walked down the side streets of the city I had lived in for almost half my life, but to which I had no true attachment beyond the convenience of having a job in it, I tried to recall lines of poetry I could apply like ointment to my linguistic wounds: "wish by spirit and if by yes," "a trout-coloured wind blows through my eyes," "Who has not sat, afraid, before his heart's curtain?" I experienced a marginal lifting of spirits.

God, or his alibi, quickly placed a pub before me. I entered, sat down at the bar, something I never do because I like corners, and ordered a double Jameson, something else I never do because it's just way too fucking expensive. I was feeling expansive, especially because I had just juxtaposed expensive and expansive in the slowly clearing landscape of my mind. Nor did I need to scan the room for beautiful women—I'd already made that kind of contact for the evening, possibly for the month. Probably for the year. I spent twenty minutes sipping my Jameson, letting the soft sting disperse throughout my body. I felt good.

"Another one?" asked the bartender, a woman about a third of my age who had obviously been hired for her body.

"Do I dare disturb the universe?"

"What?"

"In a minute there is time for decisions and revisions which a minute will reverse."

"Is that a yes?"

"That's Eliot."

She looked around, as if I'd just tried to introduce somebody who wasn't there.

"He's not here," I said, trying to be helpful.

"Do you want another double or not?"

"Not."

She moved down the bar to another customer. I moved off my stool and back out onto the street. I wondered if the woman at table number three liked poetry.

As I said, I had just begun my life, or, rather, begun to renew my acquaintance with it, having been evicted from it when I was five years old. Wordsworth and Lawrence Breavman, among too many others, had opined in their respective eloquences about vocation becoming intimation and imitation, about dulling and forgetting. My life had become a list of all the things I had lost. The longer I was on the lonesome side of the desk, the more I tried to teach my students, especially my first-year students, about the premature death of truth and beauty, words that the academy harrumphed at with *faux* righteous derision, but too many of my students couldn't understand me. When I was eighteen, I couldn't understand me, either. Teaching first-year students is like trying to speak out of Ezekiel's whirlwind—everybody can see it and hear it, but nobody really knows what it is.

‡

This is a university town, so even when you try to avoid the main streets and zigzag your way through the side streets you'll not go more than a block without passing major and minor throngs of wandering students in various stages of intoxication, whether the stimulant be drugs, alcohol, or that standard elixir of just living away from home for the first time. I remember being one of them. I remember feeling as if I had truly recaptured a kind of lost innocence laced with a brash but naïve confidence in the dividends of possibility. But those moments were simply furloughs from the academy that I did not know how to escape without fear of consequence. None of us knew any other way of being in the world; hell, we didn't know what the world was. I thought that graduating from one side of the desk to the other was, if not an escape, then a refashioning of whatever I believed the world to be. Belief, I had come to believe, was a substitute for recognition. We believe things to be true that are outside the evidence of truth.

"How academic of you," said my older brother, the fitness club manager, when I expressed this opinion while we were standing in front of the barbecue in his back yard one Sunday, tending to the burgers, beers in hand. I hated beer, but I was nursing one because I was trying to nurse my forever-fractured relationship with my brother. It was no use. I dropped my beer and punched him in the face. Then he beat the crap out of me. This was the only true way in which we ever communicated; this was a truth that was recognizable. I didn't, of course, get to expand my reference to truth by relating it to beauty, which is that you can't have the one without the other. I could have quoted Keats's "Ode on a Grecian Urn" for him, but my instinct for survival precluded such an extended observation.

One of the clusters of students I passed on one of the side streets was composed of three young males, all of whom resembled my brother when he was that age. Their voices were too loud for their bodies, as their bodies were too big and clumsy for their limited life experience. They were helplessly eighteen.

"Yeah, man, she's got preemo tits," said the first body.

"Have you done her yet?" asked the second body.

"Dude, I'd do her," offered the third body.

From a right angle came another cluster of male students, the members of which were discussing the finer points of electrical engineering. As these two clusters of young males passed each other, and as their various observations of do-able young women and modular capacitor banks (or something of the kind) intersected, I was reminded of a musical experiment that the unusual American composer Charles Ives (or it might have been his father) conducted by having two marching bands, playing different tunes, begin from opposite ends of the main street and march towards each other. The point was twofold: first, to hold on to your tune while a different, competing tune got louder and louder and then was right up inside your own; second, to hear that other tune as its own tune while still hearing your tune as its own tune.

Both these types of conversation—the discipline-specific analysis and the male hormonal-specific twaddle—were not limited, however, to the newly post-pubescent spectrum of the species. To wit:

Anonymous English professor the first: "Whitman deconstructs the Stations of the Cross, indeed all religious litanies, while at the same time reconstructing the male gaze, such that Ginsberg and his followers could not have otherwise appeared as they did a century later."

Anonymous English professor the second: "Yes, but Whitman is, at best, an unwitting deconstruction of Herbert and

Swinburne, appropriating the cultural sanctity of the former and the restrained testicularity of the latter."

And, of course, anonymous male English professor the third: "Do you have that Beacham girl in your class this semester?"

Anonymous male English professor the fourth: "The one with the killer ass and legs?"

Anonymous male English professor the fifth: "She knows what she's got and she wears the clothes to prove it."

Anonymous male English professor the fourth: "Yes, but she's got smarts."

Anonymous male English professor the third: "Are you sleeping with her, then?" (It was not considered good taste to sleep with a student who was merely physically attractive; there had to be the added incentive of reasonably intelligent conversation both before and after the act; then it could be justified.)

Anonymous male English professor the second: "Whitman was the ultimate democrat when it came to the appreciation of the human form."

Anonymous male English professor the first: "Quite."

‡

After an hour of wandering, it became clear to me that one double Jameson was not enough for the kind of evening this was turning out to be. I made my way back to the main street and availed myself of the first pub I came to. As I was waiting for my whisky to arrive, I contented myself with observing a fly looking for interesting places to land without being shooed away. It had no idea that within the month, it would be dead. It also had no idea what a sense of freedom that was.

"Hey, Professor Pepperfield—how's your evening going?"

I turned from the bar and looked to my left from where the voice had come. It belonged to one of four students who were either on their way into or out of the pub. I recognized two of them as former students. The other two might also have been former students, but there were a lot of faces that, for one reason or another, never seemed to stick in my visual memory.

"I'm waiting for my whiskey to arrive, at which point the evening will have rejuvenated itself."

I knew I probably sounded somewhat pretentious, but as I pointed out before, I was trying to re-establish my love affair with language. Besides, I was no longer in the employ of these particular students and it didn't much matter what they thought of me anymore. Three of the pairs of eyes looked at me with delicate confusion, possibly because of what I'd said, possibly because of what I was wearing; the fourth pair looked at me with recognition.

"You're not teaching this semester?" asked one of the students who did not look at me with recognition.

"Or any other semester from this point forward," I answered.

"Did you retire?"

"I'm in rehab."

The three pairs of eyes that had exhibited the aforementioned delicate confusion now shifted into the deeper waters of polite incomprehension. The fourth pair recognized a metaphor when they saw one.

"Well, see you later, then," said the voices attached to the three pairs of eyes in a stuttered chorus as they followed their bodies towards the door of the pub. The body belonging to the fourth pair of eyes stayed behind.

"There's a table over in the corner," she said, nodding her head in its direction. "Would you like to sit over there with me and have your whiskey?"

"Me" was a former female student who, at first glance, would not be considered an obviously attractive woman, but she became more beautiful as her intelligence manifested itself over the course of the semester. Her hair was a non-descript shade of brown and of a non-descript style. She wore glasses that seemed to have been chosen more for functionality than aesthetic concern. Her wardrobe attested to the same kind of choice. All of this conflicted with her name, which was Violet.

Before making our way to the corner table, she ordered a martini. She carried it in one hand as if holding a flower she was about to give someone.

"This became my drink of choice," she said, taking off her coat, which she had probably just put on a few minutes ago, "once I read *Franny and Zooey* in your class."

"You connected with Franny?"

"Doesn't every college girl?"

She slowly twirled the stem of her martini glass between the fingers of both hands.

"Do you consider yourself a girl?"

The twirling stopped. The martini glass looked surprised.

"College girl sounds less puffed up than college woman. On the other hand, my father's dating someone new and he refers to her as his girlfriend. She refers to him as her boyfriend. Some words just don't know how to grow up, I guess. So, is it true that you've retired?"

"As we grow older the world becomes stranger, the pattern more complicated of dead and living."

"I feel as if I should recognize that from somewhere," she said, beginning again to twirl the stem of her martini glass.

"Eliot," I said.

I was in an Eliot groove this evening.

"The Quartets?"

"The Quartets."

"What will you do now?" she asked.

She took a sip of her martini, watching for my answer over the rim of the glass.

"Read only what I want to read, when I want to read it. Say only the things I want to say, when I want to say them."

"I wish I could do that."

"You can."

"You forget what it's like being a student."

She wasn't chastising or challenging me; she was just speaking, taking her part in the conversation. She extracted the skewered olive from her glass and slid it off the toothpick with her teeth.

"It's because I do remember what it was like being a student that I say that."

"Was it better being a professor?"

"Marginally."

"I'm an education major. Any advice?"

She leaned back in her chair, perhaps expecting a wave of insightfully energized words to wash over her. This was the question I wanted all my students to ask me. It was also the question I most dreaded because to answer it was to present an apology, in the classical Greek sense of the word, for all the choices I had made, and especially had not made, in my life since I entered the school system. All that was left if I didn't present an apology were platitudes: "follow your heart," "be who you are," "ignore what everyone tells you." The sad thing was that all these pieces of advice had, indeed, become platitudes; their essence had been trivialized through overuse. The other problem was that too many students, unlike the young woman sipping her martini across the table from me, didn't understand what heart was; they had no idea who they were; and if they ignored what everyone told them, they wouldn't know what to do.

"You don't need my advice," I said.

"But I want it."

"I'm retired, remember?"

"Do you want me to leave you alone?"

I really needed to fart. I calculated the possibility of the ambient noise in the pub cloaking the sound of the fart; then I calculated the likelihood of it betraying itself by its smell. Nothing in life is ever a sure thing; sometimes you just have to step into the whirlpool. Fortunately, I had my second double Jameson to help me. I leaned forward slightly, as if I were merely repositioning myself in my chair, and farted. No sound—so far so good. I took a deep breath, as if punctuating the conversation. No odour. I had successfully navigated my way to the far side of the punctuation mark at the end of her question and could now answer it.

"No, you don't need to go. So, you want my advice. Have you ever read Aldous Huxley's *The Doors of Perception*?"

"No."

"He published it in 1954. It's about taking mescalin—this was long before acid became popular, long before everyone in the sixties was dropping it every weekend just to get stoned. Huxley was sincerely interested in the mind-altering aspects of the drug; he wanted to explore his own mind, his own perceptions of the world. Right near the beginning of the book, soon after he's ingested the mescalin and he's beginning to feel its effects, he talks about looking at a bouquet of flowers, at the arrangement of the flowers in the bouquet. He says, 'I was seeing what Adam had seen on the morning of his creation—the miracle, moment by moment, of naked existence.' Then somebody asked him if it was 'agreeable,' and he just said, 'neither agreeable nor disagreeable. It just *is*.' There has to be a way of seeing the world like that—without the drugs—a way of seeing ourselves in the world like that. I think we all used to be able to do that when we were little kids. If you're going to be a teacher, you have to try to get your students to see the world like that, even if you've lost the capacity yourself."

"And you think I have?"

"I don't know."

"But you have?"

"I'm afraid I may have, yes."

"Do you want to know what I think?"

She leaned into the table, her shoulders hunched over her martini, preparing herself to answer her own question.

"I do."

"I don't think we ever lose anything."

"Check back with me in thirty years and see if you still think that."

It was an unnecessarily cynical remark and I knew it. Her shoulders drooped and she sagged back in her chair.

"You were never like this in class," she said.

"I've disappointed you."

"In class you talked about the part of *Franny and Zooey* where Franny says that if you're a poet, you do something beautiful. She said that you had to leave something beautiful behind on the page. You talked about that passage as if you believed what she said. You left something beautiful behind in that class."

This was the point in the conversation, in my entire relationship with this former student who I wished could be my teacher, where I dropped the ceramic bowl that contained her image of me on the floor, shattering it into a hundred pieces that could never be put back together. I knew it because I was on my hands and knees too carefully trying to gather each shard without further damaging them. What poet could I quote her now that would fix what I had done?

> "'If when I die,
> all these moments of my life
> are nothing
> but a single silent echo
> of who I was,
> then remember me into your hands
> and wish upon me
> as I shoot across the sky
> of all the time there ever was.'"

"Eliot?"
"Pepperfield."
"It sounds like part of a longer poem."
"It is."
"What's the rest?"
"It begins:

> 'If when I die
> all the moments of my life
> are reduced to a single flash,
> like the blink of a shooting star
> or the slap of a hand on a shoulder,
> then what does it mean that I kissed you
> for the length of a sunset
> or that I cried for one whole moon
> when you left?'"

"That's beautiful."

"That's loss."

"It's still beautiful."

"To you, perhaps. You're young yet."

She looked back at me with controlled anger and resentment. Then it changed as suddenly as it began. I had stamped an irrevocable sadness in her eyes, and if there had been a cross available, I would have nailed myself to it and died a slow and necessarily painful death.

She drank back the last of her martini, put on her coat, and left.

‡

Back out on the street with my double buzz that now had an irreparable crack in it, I walked for the mere sake of walking. I didn't care about the woman at table number three, but I did care about my bespectacled former student. What I had opened up with the one, I had closed down with the other. I knew enough Jung to understand that I was dealing with anima projections and that I needed to have a serious talk with myself. There were no more students, especially of the female variety, upon whom I could deposit bits of my self-identity and pretend that I didn't know what I was doing. So many of those bits, though, were ones I stole from poems and novels and plays. I recognized myself in them and appropriated them as my own. It was I who built that cabin on Walden Pond. It was I who drove my motorcycle across the United States with my young son trying to find my former self that had been electroshocked out of me. It was I who heard the mermaids singing, each to each. It was I who pondered the black rook in the rain. It was I who contemplated the Grecian urn. It was I who constructed essay questions on all these experiences, hoping some student would help me figure out who I really was. And it was I who was called into the Chair's office to explain to him why I took various of my classes out to the river that ran through the woods at the far end of the campus and told them to build a lean-to and live in it for a week; to explain to him why they should take whatever vehicle they owned or could borrow, skip classes for a week, and drive as far as they could for three days and spend the next three days taking a different route back (one of them never did come back); to explain to him why they should sit by the fountain in the courtyard until they could hear—actually *hear*—the mermaids singing; to explain to him why I took them out in the pouring rain until we found a tree with a crow in it and just watched it (one of them got pneumonia and missed the rest of her semester); to explain to him how these were all reasonable and necessary essay topics. To promise him never to repeat such nonsense if I wanted to maintain tenure.

Too much flotsam and jetsam banging around in the cracked buzz of my double Jameson. I purchased a pack of cigarettes at the nearest convenience store and wandered about until I found a phone booth, that disappearing landmark on the new technological map of the fractured human community.

"Hi, Deborah, do you have a few minutes to talk?"

"Levi," she said like a punctuation mark somewhere between a period and a semicolon. "Who else phones me on the wrong side of midnight when he does deign to phone me at all? You do know that phones work in the daytime."

"Did I wake you?"

"No, but you are interrupting *Now, Voyager*."

"I can call back later."

"This is late enough, thank you very much. I haven't heard from you in months. How's the new semester?"

"I retired."

"Well, as I live and breathe!" She had this way of taking a worn-out phrase and resuscitating it when everyone else just walked by and looked at its crumpled Salvation Army clothed body moaning in the gutter. "When did this happen?"

I first met Deborah about fifteen years ago in my fourth-year Poetry as Practice class. She was a so-called "mature student," which meant that she was somewhere on the far side of thirty. She'd come up to talk to me after class, our conversation beginning as one between teacher and student, but quickly, and always, resolving itself into one between adults who happened to be interested in the same things, which ranged from the specifics of poetry to the generalities of being in the world to the nature of supreme beings, always with an unspoken undercurrent of what sex would be like with each other. Our conversations were composed of words that mattered, sometimes enough of them to fill a novella, other times only enough for a haiku or two. Sometimes, the most important words were the ones we didn't need to say; the ones that hid comfortably behind the spoken ones, like nests in high trees. Oh, and she was a Rabbi. After seven years of rabbinical training, which included two years in Safed, where she practised "surrendering upon the tombs," she "was guided" to become a counsellor. She preferred one-on-one to congregations.

"It was one of those last-minute decisions that was three years in the making," I said.

"And you're calling me because you need to debrief?"

"Something like that."

"Where are you?"

"In a phone booth."

"How very Levi Pepperfield of you. Still refusing to surrender to the cell phone?"

"I'm all out of white flags."

"So, did you make the proper preparations for this call?"

"Yes, I have cigarettes."

"Okay, let me just grab one from my night table here."

I could hear her stretching across the bed and opening the drawer.

"Okay, ready. Ready?"

"Ready."

"One . . . two . . . three . . . light up."

We lit our cigarettes together. I could hear the cap of her lighter click shut. Why did cigarette lighters no long have flip-top caps? We took that first long drag together. Breathed out the smoke together. We had the routine down. We smoked in silence until our cigarettes were done.

"Was it good for you?"

"It was. It's good to see things in the rear-view mirror sometimes."

"All forms of copulation are like that. So, now that we're sweaty and exhausted, if only on the planet of metaphors, are you back on the balance beam?"

"For now. Thanks."

"Good night, Levi. And I mean that. Make it good."

‡

The problem, as far as I could identify it, was that I did, indeed, fart and my shit did, indeed, smell—my anima, however, did not fart, nor did its shit smell. This problem was exacerbated by the fact that in so very few pieces in the literary canon before the second half of the twentieth century did any character, however major or minor, confessional or omniscient, fart or shit. Leaving aside Chaucer and Rabelais, there is a significant lacuna with regard to bodily functional profanity until we get to Ginsberg, who refers to the smell of asshole; to Richard Brautigan, who writes of how a fart smells at 1:03 in the morning; and to Leonard Cohen's *Beautiful Losers*, in which F. is burdened with literal and metaphorical constipation. William Burroughs is a canon unto himself in this regard.

The other problem with my anima was that it had female parts. When I first taught *Beautiful Losers*, I was fine reading out loud passages about fucking a saint, but when it came to reading the word "cunt" out loud, I couldn't do it. I got all the way up to the word and then paused, awkwardly. Deborah, sitting in the front row, said it out loud for me, with all the nonchalance of someone ordering a latte. This collision of my reticence and her easeful it's-just-another-word attitude made it clear to me that I needed to expand my sensibilities in directions heretofore unexplored. Hence the occasional cigarette sex over the phone.

The evening was now well and truly night, and the air threatened cold rather than teasing me with it. Soon, all the pubs would be closed, and if I wanted warmth and lubrication I would have to rely on all-night cafés. Besides, another double Jameson would, I was sure, nudge me over the line between buzz, cracked or not, and depression. Like Cohen and Plath, Baudelaire and

Blake, Keats and Eliot, I was—and am—a chronic depressive. Unlike them, I did not and do not have the creative capacity as a writer to staunch the emotional bleeding, though my bespectacled former student would, now reluctantly, beg to differ.

I wandered my way down to the campus where I had not been since I officially retired just over four months ago. I had been pretty sure that I would never set foot on its academically hallowed grounds again. I was fortified with a safe dose of Jameson, which allowed me a perspective of distance, such that I could walk the grounds with a pleasant detachment, observing the environment as one who had just stepped off a spaceship with a headful of benign curiosity. It was one of those deliciously rare campuses that has a river running through it, and it gave the old limestone buildings a natural magnificence that they would not otherwise have had. Not only did I teach here for most of my career, but I had been a student here, as well. I had, therefore, a kind of incestuous relationship with the place. But tonight I had new eyes and it was a book I was reading for the first time.

Chapter One was set in the women's residence, just the other side of the river. It was there that a beautiful young woman lived, the woman whom the protagonist of the story believed he was in love with. The reader knows, though, that our young protagonist is mistaking infatuation for love, as everyone does the first time, and, sometimes, the second and third time.

Chapter Two, three years later, sees the young man walking along the river with a different young woman who is waiting for him to stop and take her in his arms and kiss her for the first time. She says all the words she can say to try to make this happen, even using the word kiss in an abstracted sort of way, but the young man, though he doesn't know it himself, has learned to deflect such encounters. He will also not realize for many years afterwards that he has unwittingly and unfortunately inoculated himself against the surrender that makes life worth living.

By the time I get to Chapter Three, I am walking the long slow hill, at the top of which sits the original building of the university. I remember walking out of this building one December evening after my last exam of the fall semester, the snow falling like soundless fragments of some faraway mystical explosion. I didn't know how to articulate truth that night, but beauty was everywhere, even inside me. I felt I could drift up into the night sky if I tilted my head back far enough.

Just as I get to the top of the hill I see him coming towards me—Barkley Forrester, Chair of the English Department, a man whom I could never quite consider to be an actual human being. I'm sure he considered me in the same light. What the hell was he doing here at this time of night? He was about twenty steps away, that awkward distance that you know will too slowly and too quickly be collapsed, demanding of you some sort of greeting that acknowledges familiarity but is seasoned with contempt. I do not want to speak to this man.

"Mr. Pepperfield," he says, never having allowed himself to address me familiarly as Levi or respectfully as Professor or Doctor. "I didn't expect to see you back here so soon. Or at this time of night. Or dressed in quite that manner."

"Good evening, Mr. Forrester. Nor did I expect to see you."

We were, the both of us, suspended between movement and stillness.

"Good night," I said, and continued on my way.

I owed him nothing, especially since he had just ruined the peacefulness of my wandering. He had sabotaged that pleasant detachment in which I was basking, and I hated him for it. From the dark edges of my fragile ego, anger came rushing like blood through every vein in my body. That's how it always happened. It was never a slow burn for me. I had, though, over the years, developed a technique whereby I could forestall it from overwhelming me for hours and sometimes even days, as it used to do. I took three or four very deep breaths and time-travelled back to my five-year-old self sitting against the garage door, facing down the long driveway into the morning sun as it rose over the treetops on the far side of the road, feeling its heat suddenly warm my body, which, just the moment before, shivered in the early summer morning chill.

I waited for a few minutes, completed my walk to the top of the hill, standing before the great doors of the great building, turned and looked back down the hill whence I had come.

‡

At the gates of the campus, on the main road that went into the city centre, squatted a shoebox-shaped diner that catered to students twenty-four-seven, but was democratic enough that certain faculty members who knew how to, could feel *à l'aise dans sa peau*, and students didn't feel intimidated by their presence. We were all just humans when we walked in that door. It was a simple design, with booths on either side of the single central aisle. There was enough light to see what you were eating and who was across the table from you, but not so much that you could make out those obscure facial defects in each other that only an obsessive eye could find. It was never clear to me exactly where the light came from. My waitress was a motherly-aged woman who called students and professors alike "dear," without any trace of condescension, and generally thought of us all as lost and delicate orphans who would be spiritually crippled without her attention.

"Coffee, neat, with a side of cinnamon toast, dear?"

She knew every person's "regular" by heart. If she were a student, she could ace any multiple-choice exam in any discipline.

"How are your classes this semester?" she asked, placing my coffee and toast on the table.

"No more classes. I just retired."

"Well, that's wonderful. You deserve a nice long break after a job well done for so many years. You know you're always welcome to keep coming back here. You're one of us, dear."

Of course, she had no idea whether I had done my job well or not, but she assumed the best about everybody. And when she called me "one of us," I felt a soft stab of worthiness.

The coffee was as good as coffee that isn't perked can be. It was the last place in the city where you could order coffee without any extraneous adjectives attached to it.

Chapter Four presented itself to me as I bit into my cinnamon toast.

"Hope you don't mind doing the interview here, but it's a welcoming place to start, don't you think?"

So said Professor Collinson to the young applicant to fill the vacancy in the English Department as he ordered two coffees and two orders of cinnamon toast—"You like cinnamon toast? It's comfort food, don't you think?" He was always asking the applicant what he thought, though as a rhetorical rather than a probing question. He referred very briefly to the applicant's CV and to the fact that he'd done his undergrad here, though they had never crossed paths in the classroom. With his first sip of coffee, Professor Collinson started talking about Whitman, as if he were picking up a conversation they had already begun.

"When I first read *Leaves of Grass* I was seventeen—it was before I even began university. It wasn't a text I'd studied in high school, either. I just saw it in a bookstore one day and the drawing of Whitman on the cover caught my eye. It was one of those books you read as if you'd written it yourself, you know?"

The applicant did know. He launched into the story of his first, unsuccessful, doctoral dissertation on Whitman and Brautigan, after which he and Professor Collinson traded favourite passages from both writers like two kids trading observations about their new grade six teacher who was the best and most interesting teacher they'd ever had in all their six years of schooling. By the time they'd finished their coffee and toast, ordered and lazed their way through a second order of both, Professor Collinson reached across the table and shook the applicant's hand. "You're hired, Levi," he said.

Two days later, they were back in the diner with two other English profs, talking about *The Catcher in the Rye*, as if they'd all personally hung out with Holden Caulfield; about Eliot's *Four Quartets*, as if they'd each written one of them; about *Keep the Aspidistra Flying*, as if Gordon Comstock might walk into the diner looking for a place to smoke his last cigarette. The newly hired English professor thought he'd just walked through the pearly gates and realized that heaven was right here on Earth the whole time.

They were all older than this new professor and had all come through the ranks before the advent of literary theory. Then, as each new recruit joined the department, they could feel the chill of theory divorced from intuition descending upon them. Conversations, such as they were—more like the exchange of dissertation fragments about Derrida and Lacan and Foucault, rather than enthusiasms about Salinger and Eliot and Orwell—took place in the hallways outside office doors. There was no time or desire to relax among the beauty of words, rather than the analysis of terms, at the diner. Whatever truth and beauty were, they were losing their force, and one by one, those profs who had welcomed the applicant into the department retired, some before the new academia had sucked them dry, some prematurely shrivelled. They all left, more with a sense of loss than of anger. The new guy ended up experiencing both. Thus went the later chapters of the book.

My coffee and cinnamon toast drunk and eaten, I decided to lay the book down for a while.

‡

Guys like me don't know how to get married. The longer we lose ourselves in literature, the less real the possibility of cohabiting with a flesh-and-blood woman becomes. The best affairs I've had have been with Dorothea Brooke, Catherine Earnshaw, Irene Adler, and Franny Glass. Of course, there are all the women on the covers of the Richard Brautigan books, and though they are real women, they still inhabit a plane of existence that I don't have a map for. Between all the aforementioned and my anima, I've been pretty much out of circulation in the real-world lending library. You can understand, then, that my foray into the halls of speed-dating was a breakthrough of sorts.

I was on the downslope of my Jameson buzz, I had sideskirted depression, and now I found myself in the downtown core at three o'clock in the morning trying, in spite of my questionable sartorial state, to look like someone who was not destitute or deranged, which most of the people left on the streets at this time of night seemed to be. They were all men in various stages of bedragglement, and I could imagine being any one of them. For all I knew, they could all be serious writers researching new stories or beaten down by the very stories they had already written.

"Hey buddy . . . hey buddy, spare a quarter for a cup of coffee?"

He certainly qualified as bedraggled—unkempt hair, splotchy growth of facial hair, knee-length coat that looked as if it had been slept in longer than it ever wanted to be, and shoes that had a long-ago memory of being dress shoes and didn't fit his feet properly.

"There's a place where you can get a cup of coffee for a quarter?" I asked him before I could censor myself.

"Okay, ya got a coupla bucks you can spare for a cup of coffee?"

His eyes weren't glazed over, he didn't smell, and he didn't seem to be carrying a weapon, so I offered to take him into whatever place was open and buy him a cup of coffee. The place we found was probably the only other eating establishment in the city that sold just plain coffee, though I suspected it was made from beans that were left over on the floor and swept up at the end of the day to be sold specifically to establishments like this one.

"Here," he said, extracting a beaten-up paperback from his coat pocket. "I can sell you this to pay for the coffee."

It was a biography of Eva Braun.

"Have you read this?" I asked.

"Sure."

"What's it about?"

He picked it up off the table where he had just placed it and squinted at the cover for a second or two.

"Eva Braun," he said.

He ordered a piece of pie along with his coffee. I suppose he figured the book was worth the added victual.

"What's your name?" I asked.

"What's it matter?"

"I don't suppose it does in the long run."

The restaurant, which seemed like a rather grand term for the place we were in, was lit with fluorescent lights so that everything was covered in a wounded white light. Besides the waitress, who was too young and too pretty to be working in this kind of place at this time of night, we were the only two people there. When our orders arrived, he picked his slab of pie off the plate, leaned his head back, and dumped the whole thing into his gaping mouth.

"Bring him some pie, too," he called to the waitress, who was now back behind the counter.

Bits of partially masticated pie sprayed from his mouth as he spoke.

"It's okay, I don't want any."

"Sure you do."

The look in his eyes shifted from dull to weirdly sharp.

"Bring him some pie," he called again to the waitress, this time more like an angry shout.

"Really . . ." I said, at which point he vaulted out of the booth and stomped towards the counter where the waitress tensed up with fear.

"Goddam pie!" he yelled, now on the far side of control.

She didn't move quickly enough for him. He reached into his coat pocket and pulled out a gun. Clearly, I was wrong about him being weaponless. He clomped his way around the end of the counter, his gun trained at her head the whole time, until he was standing an arm's length away from her, he at one end of the arm, the gun and the waitress's head at the other.

"Take off that dress," he said.

"It's okay, mister," she sputtered. "I'll get you the pie."

"Fuck the pie! Take off that dress."

"Please, mister."

I slid myself out of the booth as non-threateningly as I could and stood up. He swung his gun arm wildly toward me and pulled the trigger. The bullet splatted into the wall behind me. I didn't know if he meant to miss me or not. He immediately swung his arm back towards the waitress. I couldn't think of any line of poetry that was appropriate to this particular circumstance.

"Take off the fuckin' dress."

His voice seemed calmer, but it was a calm that didn't believe in itself. The waitress slid her arms out of the top part of her smock and shimmied it down past her waist. I could only see the top half of her standing there with her bra on.

"Please, mister, don't do anything, please."

He started to laugh a deep belly laugh that shook his whole body.

"Don't do anything, she says," and he kept laughing, almost unable to control himself. "Whadya think I'm gonna do, eh, sweetheart?"

His laugh stopped as abruptly as it began.

"Bra and panties," he said, too slowly, waving the gun up and down the length of her body.

The waitress looked towards me for some kind of help.

"Hey, buddy," I tried, "why don't you just take the money from the till and we can call it a night? You can have the rest of my cash, too," I said, pulling my wallet out of my coat pocket. His gun arm swung back towards me. A more measured pull of the trigger this time. He missed again.

"Okay, okay," she said and unhooked her bra.

I was ashamed to be looking at her naked breasts and thinking how beautiful they were. Then I could see her making the motions to slide her panties off. When she stood up straight again, he looked her up and down with an almost angelic smile on his face, as if he were remembering something beautiful. He shook his head, settling deeper into the memory. His gun arm fell to his side. He turned and walked out of the restaurant.

"Jesus, are you okay?" I said, rushing towards the counter.

"Don't come near me," she cried.

She wasn't wholly convinced that I wasn't some sort of accomplice.

"It's okay, I'm an English professor."

I waited until she had put all her clothes back on.

"Is there anything I can do?" I asked from my side of the counter.

"I think you've done enough, don't you?"

"What do you mean?"

"You brought that lunatic in here to rape me."

"Listen, I've never met the guy before. I offered to buy him a cup of coffee, that's all."

"Why should I believe you?"

"Because he shot at me. Twice."

"But he didn't hit you."

I felt that I needed to apologize for not being dead, or at least seriously wounded.

"And he didn't rape you. You're okay. We both survived."

"He didn't rape me?" she yelled at me. "What's your definition of rape?"

In the circumstance, there was no good answer to that question.

"Do you want me to call the police?"

"Don't . . . call . . . anybody."

She measured the words out like a countdown.

"Fine."

I felt absurdly defensive.

"I'd like to remind you that I was shot at. Twice. I thought he was going to kill me."

"But he didn't."

"And he didn't . . ."

"Rape me?"

She reached under the counter and her hand came up with a large long knife in it.

"Let's see how you like it. Take off your clothes."

She walked around the edge of the counter and stepped carefully towards me.

"You don't really want to do this," I countered.

"Don't I? Take them off."

I took off my paisley scarf and corduroy jacket, then paused, hoping she would reconsider. Her eyes and her posture suggested otherwise. I pulled off my Bob Dylan tee shirt. I paused again. No reconsideration, not even taking my less than appealing torso into account. So, it was off with the one-size-too-big jeans and my boxer shorts, which, for some ridiculous reason, given the circumstances, I was glad were clean. It's hard to describe what this de-robing felt like. Humiliation wasn't the right word; neither was fear or anger, or even helplessness. It was, ridiculously, the closest I had ever gotten to an out-of-body experience. There I was, looking down on my naked body, except for my baseball cap, shoes, and socks, and it was not a pretty sight.

"Rape: forcible interference, violation, from the Latin *rapio, rapere, rapui, raptum*," she said. "To seize, snatch, tear away. Still think I wasn't raped, mister English professor?"

"Okay, I get it."

I retrieved my boxers and put them back on.

"I didn't say you could do that yet."

"I understand, but this has gone far enough."

I pulled on my pants. She swung the knife at me. It was not a calculated swing. The knife slashed my forearm, but just. Still, it began to bleed enough to scare the shit out of both of us.

"Oh my god," she said, dropping the knife and bringing her hands up to her face.

"First-aid kit?" I pleaded.

She ran back behind the counter and into the back room. After the sound of boxes being tossed around and heavy clanky things falling on the floor, she emerged, First-aid kit in hand. She sat me down in the nearest booth, opened the kit, found some sort of iodine-like substance, but realized the blood needed to be cleaned up first so that she could see the wound clearly. She grabbed my good arm with one of her hands, closed the lid of the First-aid kit and picked it up with the other one of her hands and hurried me to the washroom. Minutes later, my arm cleaned and bandaged, we were sitting on the floor side by side, slumped against the wall next to the sink. Our shoulders were almost touching. We were staring straight ahead. It had been a long time without words.

"Is this the men's or the women's?" I asked.

"Women's."

"Oh, yeah," I said, realizing there were no urinals. "Clean."

"Yeah."

"Levi," I said.

"April," she said.

"I've never met an April before. And I've met a lot of women. Students."

"I was born in April. My mother is terminally British. You get the picture. You really are an English professor?"

"Was."

"Classics student," she said.

We were still looking straight ahead; our shoulders were still almost touching.

"You always do the night shift?" I asked.

"Just filling in for somebody on holiday. My first night shift."

"Last one?"

"Pretty sure."

"I'm sorry."

"It's not that great a job."

"No, I meant I'm sorry about what happened."

"Yeah."

"Anybody here?" came a voice from somewhere out in the restaurant.

"Fuck off!" yelled April.

A few seconds of silence followed by the sound of the restaurant door closing. We looked at each other and began to laugh a laugh of shared release.

"I really am sorry," April said.

"I'm going to get my tee shirt and jacket. It's cold in here."

"I can't believe I did that," April said, putting her hand gently on my bandaged arm.

"Let's pretend it never happened."

"I don't think I can do that."

"Writers pretend all the time. That's all literature is."

"But stuff happens in literature. Writers pretend that stuff happens, not that stuff never happened. I wish this never happened."

We sat there on the bathroom floor, hunched against the wall, our shoulders almost touching, considering the vagaries of wish fulfillment. Five, maybe ten, minutes later, we went back into the restaurant, where I put on my tee shirt and jacket and paisley scarf.

"You dress . . . oddly."

"It's a long story."

Then we sat on stools at the counter, side by side, staring at nothing in particular on the other side of the counter, waiting for nothing else to happen.

I've spent my whole life waiting. That's how we Christians are raised—waiting for the judgment day, waiting for Jesus to come back, waiting for revelation, waiting for all this to be over so we can live in heaven in eternal bliss. In school, you wait to graduate elementary school, then you wait to graduate high school, then you wait to graduate university, then you wait to retire, then you wait to die. You fill up each of these stages with various distractions, but always, you are waiting for something better, and losing things along the way. All the moments of waiting fit into each other like Russian dolls. Waiting for deliverance. Waiting while we wait for deliverance. Waiting while we're waiting while we wait for deliverance.

"Let's smash all these Russian dolls," I said.

"What?" April said.

"Let's go out and make some truth and beauty."

She began to wonder if her original sense of my character as being an accomplice of a crazy person might not be correct.

"Retired English professor stuff," I said, sliding off my stool, and walking towards the door. I pulled it open.

"Wait."

The word pulled my hand off the door. I turned and looked back at her.

"It might be retired waitress stuff, too."

"This *is* your last night. You said so yourself."

"You think I should?"

I shrugged my shoulders in a "why not" fashion. I was oozing recklessness. Perhaps it was the blood loss.

"Let me get my coat."

Lights turned out, door closed and locked behind us, we walked out into burgeoning four in the morning.

"I feel as if I'm beginning an odyssey."

"How very classical of you."

"I'm trying to apply my learning."
"You're returning home then?"
"Depends what you mean by home."

The restaurant slowly receded into our metaphysical rear-view mirror. Our words were launched into the world in puffs of white vapour, only to disappear before they could attach themselves to anything.

"The place you started out from," I answered. "The place you want to be when you're not there."

"Odysseus spent ten years trying to get home to Penelope. Maybe home is another person."

"Do you think he was content to live out the rest of his days in domestic bliss with Penelope? Tennyson and Kazantzakis thought he could never get the urge for adventure out of his blood."

"Home versus adventure—is that the choice we have to make?"

"If you put it that way . . ."
"You put it that way."
"Tennyson and Kazantzakis put it that way."
"I thought you wanted to make some truth and beauty. That's what you offered."
"I did."
"Well?"
"It was a rhapsodic utterance."
"Do you mean that to be a synonym for untruth?"
"I was overwhelmed by a moment of beauty."
"What moment was that?"
"It was in my head."
"Where is it now?"
"I don't have a good answer for that."
"Home or adventure? Which one are you after?"
"I don't have a good answer for that, either."
She stopped.
"I'm going back to the restaurant."
"But I thought you were going to quit."
"I am. I'm going to go back and give my official notice."

"What about you? Home or adventure?"

"The journey home *is* the adventure." She walked a few steps away from me, stopped, and turned to look at me. "I'm sorry about your wound."

‡

It felt good to be wounded. It proved I existed. It proved that I actually got in the way of the universe for a moment. By four in the morning it seemed that even the street people had gone to ground. I felt as if I were the only living person in the city; the streets were all my own. I dispensed with sidewalks and high-wired the white lines down the middle of the main street. Which is when the cop car pulled up beside me, and the cop in the passenger seat requested politely, but firmly, that I step to the side of the road. The car pulled over in front of me and the two cops stepped out of the car.

"You got some identification?" asked cop the first.

"I'm Levi Pepperfield, recently retired professor of English, walking wounded."

"Do you have a wallet with some identification in it?" continued cop the first.

"My word isn't good enough?"

"Are you on any narcotics right now?" asked cop the second.

"Two double shots of Jameson and some literary mescaline."

"I think you'd better come with us," said cop the second.

"Come on," I countered. "Do I look like a homeless person?"

Given my attire, that was an unfortunate question to pose.

"Would a homeless person be this articulate?" I tried to redeem myself. "Could a homeless person quote Wordsworth: 'And now it would content me to yield up those lofty hopes awhile, for present gifts of humbler industry?' Would a homeless person be able to afford Jameson? Would a homeless person know how to use anaphora?"

"Just come along with us," repeated cop the second.

"There's no one else on the streets—whom am I disturbing?"

"Right now, you're disturbing us," said cop the first.

Cop the first took my left arm, the good one, and cop the second took my right arm, the wounded one, and carefully stuffed me into the back seat of the cop car. At the station, they escorted me into an interview room where, after ten minutes or so, another cop came in and sat down across the table from me. I had surrendered my wallet to cop the first at the desk before being seated in the interview room.

"You're Levi Pepperfield. You live at 1125 Frobisher Road. You're a faculty member at Riverdene University. What were you doing walking down the middle of Charter Street at four o'clock in the morning?"

"Experiencing an unexpected freedom. There wasn't a car in sight; there wasn't another living person within shouting distance of me and I just decided it would be interesting to walk down the middle of the road. Are you going to charge me with jaywalking?"

"You told the officers you were recently retired. Is that true?"

"It is. I'm just trying to explore my new life."

"You also said you were 'walking wounded.' What's that about?"

"No one gets to this age unscathed."

"If I release you now, will you give me your word that you'll go straight home from here—on the sidewalks?"

"I give you my word. Better yet, I'll give you these words:

> 'Give we the hills our equal prayer:
> Earth's breezy hills and heaven's blue sea;
> We ask for nothing further here
> But our own hearts and liberty.'

"I can't remember the poet . . ."

"If you're trying to convince me that you're clear-headed and capable of being released on your own recognizance, I'm not sure you're choosing the best way to do that."

"Fine."

He shoved himself back from the table, file folder in hand, and stood up. I did the same, except that I didn't have a file folder.

"I'm retiring next month," he said.

He turned towards the door and then turned back to face me.

"What did it feel like?" he asked.

"Retiring?"

"Walking down the middle of Charter Street at four o'clock in the morning."

"It felt good."

He smiled a smile in which resignation and recognition fought for control. He held the door open for me. As I walked past him I put my hand on his shoulder, then walked back out into the night, which was now early morning.

‡

How did I become an English professor? There are, of course, the obvious reasons that have to do with doing well in English in high school, continuing to do well in university, and then falling into professorship because there was nowhere else to fall, but the odd thing was that I never had any books as a kid. My parents bought me tinker toys and baseball gloves and the like, but they never bought me any books. I read only the textbooks from school. I didn't even read the newspaper, not even the sports section, even though I was mildly interested in sports, mostly because of my older brother, and he was only a role model by default. As I said, I did well in high school English but then I did well in all my courses—I was a bright kid.

It was in my first year at Riverdene University that I took an English course, during the poetry section of which we read some of the so-called canonical poets and skimmed through some of the ones who, though not in the canon, might arrive there soon if enough English professors who made extra money by editing poetry anthologies decided to include them. Such a poet was Mrs. Oakes-Smith (1806-1893), so was she listed in the earlier anthologies. Her first name was Elizabeth. The poem that shifted me from simple, run-of-the-mill bright kid to English major and future professor was a sonnet called "An Incident:"

> A simple thing, yet chancing as it did,
> When life was bright with its illusive dreams,
> A pledge and promise seemed beneath it hid
> The ocean lay before me, tinged with beams
> That lingering draped the west, a wavering stir;
> And at my feet down fell a worn grey quill:
> An eagle, high above the darkling fir,
> With steady flight, seemed there to take his fill
> Of that pure ether breathed by him alone.
> O noble bird! why didst thou loose for me
> Thy eagle plume? still unessayed, unknown,
> Must be that pathway fearless winged by thee:
> I ask it not, no lofty flight be mine;
> I would not soar like thee, in loneliness to pine!

The mystery of it, the moment of promise and possibility denied at the very end, the sadness—I recognized it all, the truth and beauty of it all. It was the first time I realized that other people were writing my life for me, had been writing it for me before I even arrived on this plane of existence. They knew me before there was a me. I became an English major and then an English professor because I was trying to find out who I was.

The question confronting me now that I was retired was twofold: was I abandoning my search, as Elizabeth Oakes-Smith, in her own way, had done, and if I was to continue my search, could I do it without the give and take of the classroom? Of course, I could, and would, keep reading, but I had to admit that the intercourse with my students often opened up passages of literature to me in ways that simple solo reading could not. I was a spontaneous teacher; I thought on my feet rather than arriving at lectures with file folders full of notes. When I held forth in class, I was most often using my students as I used Jameson—to liberate ideas that lived inside me like birds in cages. Angelou's caged bird might sing of freedom, but my caged birds were many and they would not sing until released. Even then, most of the songs they sang could be heard only by me, and that was because I could recognize them, where most of my students could not. What if I could no longer learn without teaching?

‡

By the time I arrived at Deborah's house, the sun was just blurring the horizon. I knocked on her door.

"Jesus, Levi, I've hardly been to bed. And we've already smoked our cigarettes."

In spite of the obvious inconvenience I was causing her, she gave me a warm lingering hug. I could feel her large breasts, which always seemed to precede her into the classroom when I first knew her, push into my chest. I remember, too, that it took several appearances in my class during that semester before I realized that her immediately apparent square shape belied the curves to be found in her breasts and her legs.

"Okay, Levi," she said as she released me, "before you explain why you're here, at the ungodly hour that you're here, I'm going to take advantage of my sleep-deprived state and make a new rule in our relationship. The rule is this: whenever you show up at my house at sunrise when I've been watching *Now, Voyager* until the wee hours of the morning, interrupted by a phone call from you involving the ritual smoking of cigarettes, you have to fuck me into oblivion. Do we have a deal?"

Deborah and I had never slept together—we had never even kissed—although recently we had begun to make fleeting references to the possibility of those things. I thought it would ruin our friendship; she had opined on more than one occasion that it would "season" it.

"Geez, Deborah, I . . ."

"Good, we have a deal."

"Are rabbis allowed to . . ."

"I'm a human, Levi. A human woman."

She took my hand and pulled me behind her into her bedroom. She undressed me without once taking her eyes off mine. A smile of anticipation tempered with clear intention curved the edges of her lips. She paused for a split second when she saw the bandage on my arm, but decided to wait until later to inquire into the history of it. When I was naked, she pulled her nightdress, her only article of clothing, over her head and threw it to the side. Then she rose on tiptoes, put her arms around my neck, and kissed me. For a long time. I eased her backwards onto her bed and proceeded to fuck her into oblivion, as requested.

I have fucked my share of women in my day, but this was the most unfettered fuck I had ever experienced. If I had lost my virginity with this kind of intensity and desire-become-surrender, I would have never been able to focus on anything else for the rest of my life. Lying beside each other with the sun now streaming through her bedroom window, she reached over to her night table, opened the drawer, took out a pack of cigarettes and a lighter. She extracted a cigarette, put it between her lips, and handed me the lighter. I lit her cigarette. She extracted a second cigarette, handed it to me, and lit it.

"I've been waiting my whole life for this," she said, blowing a lungful of smoke into the air.

"I'm flattered," I said with the appropriate balance of honesty and playfulness.

"No, I mean really. That was my first time."

"Having someone light you up a cigarette after sex?"

"Having someone light me up."

"You mean . . ."

She smiled coyly.

"You mean I've just deflowered you?"

"Not as poetically a nuanced description as I've come to expect from you, but yes, you have. And no, you don't have to convert to Judaism and marry me."

"I wasn't . . ."

"Yes, you were. I know you. Now, I *really* know you."

I felt as if she'd just returned something I'd lost.

"Didn't the guy in *Now, Voyager* put both cigarettes in his mouth, light them, then hand one to the woman."

"In the movie, yes—four times, but in the book, this is how they did it—without the sex, of course. This way preserves the romance but denies the hierarchy of power. By the by, you seem to prefer my breasts to all other parts of my body—not that I'm complaining, you understand, given that right now every part of my body feels quite appreciated."

I did spend much of my time with one or the other of her nipples in my mouth. She had magnificent breasts.

"Isaac the Blind, a medieval Jewish mystic, said that 'the inner, subtle essences can be contemplated only by sucking, not by knowing.' Just thought you might appreciate that. So, what would you like to talk about?"

"I think I just forgot all the words I ever knew."

"Thank you. It was that good for me, too."

We smoked our cigarettes wordlessly.

"What's with the bandaged arm?" she asked, our cigarette butts safely in an ashtray.

"Knife fight."

"Did you win?"

"It was a draw."

She snuggled against me, her head on one shoulder, her arm reaching around to embrace the other one.

"You've known me as a teacher and as a more or less normal human being now for about fifteen years, and I was wondering . . ."

"May I just interject here that we should have been lying in this depleted condition much sooner than now?"

"You may."

"Thank you. Continue."

"Do you think I can survive without teaching? You know how spontaneity in the classroom is how I figure things out—do you think I can keep figuring things out when I don't have a classroom to do it in anymore?"

"How did you used to figure things out before you were a teacher?"

"I think there was a time when I didn't need to figure things out—when things just made sense all on their own."

"When was the last time you remember knowing that?"

"Probably when I was five years old."

"Sounds like you picked up a *klipah* along the way since then."

I recognized a Jewish term when I heard it.

"The first creation story in Genesis, where God creates the world out of the watery chaos, is more interesting and more complicated than it seems. In the Kabbalah we begin with *Ein Sof*, which, for lack of a better translation, means something like Infinite Nothingness, but at the same time it's a presence that fills that nothingness. It's the radical transcendence of *Adonai*. Creation happens in three parts. First, *Ein Sof* draws in its breath, contracting the universe, which is *Ein Sof* itself. This is the *tsimtsum* and it's done in order to open up a space outside of the *Ein Sof* for creation to come into being. The second stage happens when the *Ein Sof* then sends out a pure and radiant light from its divine consciousness into seven vessels, but this light is so overwhelming that the vessels can't contain it, and they and the light are shattered—*shevirah*. The sparks fall down through lesser planes of consciousness, including our human consciousness of space and time. Some of these sparks get covered in a kind of husk, which we call a *klipah*. There are all kinds of interpretations of what a *klipah* is—some of them have to do with versions of Adam's wife before Eve was created; some Talmudists say that the *lee-leeth*—screeching owl—in Isaiah's deserted wasteland, 'no kingdom is there,' refers to her, but in any case, and to put this in the context of your problem, the *klipah* is like a husk or second skin that captures your body or your spirit and imprisons it so that it can't manifest its true nature, which is a pure and unsullied consciousness, like one of the original divine sparks. So, you have to peel off and banish your *klipah*."

"Can a guy who was raised Catholic do that?"

"I'm sure there's some Catholic version of the *klipah*. The name doesn't matter; the mythology doesn't matter. The fact of the matter matters."

"You said there were three parts; what's the third part?"

"The third part is *tikkun olam*—repairing the world. It's our job as human beings to gather those shards of broken light and restore them to divinity. For you, however, there is also *tikkun ha'nafesh*—repairing of the soul. You might want to start there."

After a second visit to oblivion, with the requisite lighting and smoking of cigarettes, I was exhausted in all the ways that a man of my age could be exhausted. More than anything, I wanted—needed—to sleep, but I couldn't get what Deborah said out of my mind. The Catholic *klipah*, I figured, was like a thief who not only stole your essence, but moved into your head to fuck the rest of your life. I remembered an exact instance of this happening. I was in grade four, and on one of the weekly visits the priest paid to our school, he explained venial sins. He said, for example, that swearing was a venial sin. I was okay with that; I could refrain from swearing easily enough. But then he said that to even think of a swear word was the same as swearing. For weeks afterward, I couldn't stop thinking of swear words—they just kept drifting into my head like a plague of locusts across the face of the earth. I was sure I was going to hell. Hell, I was already in hell.

While I was taking this stumble down memory lane, Deborah had extricated herself from the tangle of sheets and gone off to the kitchen. Naked. She returned with a cup of coffee in each hand. Naked. She gave me one of them as she arranged herself under the sheets once again. I put my lips to the edge of the cup, feeling the heat and smelling the aroma of the coffee. I took a sip.

"Is this perked?"

"I remember you saying somewhere around our first meeting when we were no longer student and teacher that you preferred perked coffee. I remember you bemoaning the fact that it was impossible to get perked coffee in a restaurant or café, so you did most of your dedicated coffee drinking at home where you had a percolator that you had brought from your parents' home when you first moved out and went to university. Sometime after that conversation I went on a quest for a percolator. I wanted to see what all the fuss was about. Now I'm hooked, too."

"We may have to get married after all," I said.

"Never make decisions like that without protective clothing."

After the benediction of perked coffee, we did put on our protective clothing and went out for breakfast.

"Levi, about your choice of wardrobe. Should I ask?"
"Trying to turn over a new leaf."
"What kind of tree were you standing under?"
"One with a compromised identity."
"I'd think about calling a good arborist."

Over eggs benedict, for her, and corned beef hash, for me, I explained my newest plan of action, a direct consequence of her very recent mystical interpretation of my situation. I thanked her for that, and for the way in which she managed to say a good deal of it with her naked body.

"Give 'em hell," she said an hour later as we hugged each other goodbye.

‡

It was the heart of morning out on the streets. There was a crispness in the air that signalled fall, my favourite season, probably because it blessed us all—all of us who were subject to the academic year—with the possibility of new beginning. The pure white pages of Hilroy scribblers anticipated the neat cursive of inked letters and diagrams, the edges of Pink Pearl erasers were still pristine, the tips of yellow Eagle pencils were perfectly pointed, the jars of Skrip ink waited to be dipped into by the shiny nibs of Schaeffer fountain pens. Even after these Septembers had been unmasked and their deceitfulness nailed to the walls we had built around ourselves, we helplessly held on to the echo of possibility, of renewal.

But this September, the very one I was walking the streets of at this moment, reminded me of a five-year-old's September; perhaps it, like me, would recover itself. "Begone, *klipah* of September! Begone, *klipah* of Levi Pepperfield!"

And then, revelation—one of those revelations that, when it comes to you, makes you wonder how you had not known it before, it was so obvious: no writer writes their poems or plays or stories or novels with the intention that those works of art be vivisected in the academy. Writers write for themselves and for human beings, not for academics. Walt Whitman would probably chase everyone out of the classroom if he knew what we were doing to his poetry in the "hallowed halls." I only had to recall his "When I Heard the Learn'd Astronomer" to prove this point. Ginsberg did readings at campuses, but only as an act of subversion, to try to convince the young members of his audience to remain human in the face of all those academic forces that were trying to redefine humanity as something that should be commodified. All good writing, writing that is true and beautiful, scours the written human vocabulary for new and inventive ways of saying, "I fart and my shit smells." I wished I had one more class—one more class to walk in and reveal this to my students.

☦

I had been up for a long time, but I was long past the point of being able to lie down and go to sleep. I was in a heightened state of awareness and I was looking for things to be aware of. I felt like the trumpet in Charles Ives's "The Unanswered Question," the question being, "How do I re-Levi myself?"

I walked back to my house and went in only long enough to change into less ridiculous clothes and to grab an armful of my high school yearbooks and take them out into the light of this new September day. On a bench in a park in the middle of town next to a five-street intersection, I opened the first one, wondering if the pages might not crumble like dust the way a mummified corpse does when exposed to air for the first time in thousands of years. Photos of students at their lockers or in the hallways between classes or watching football games in the snow, all taken surreptitiously by some candid yearbook photographer; photos of students mugging for the camera, so intensely present in themselves, having no sense that that moment would be launched into the future to circle all our lives like satellites preserving data forever; individual mug shots for each class, faces smiling too confidently or too reluctantly, some of them evidence that the click of the camera happened too soon; group photos of the football and basketball teams and the cheerleaders, junior and senior; photos of our teachers, looking as if they'd been taken in a different space-time continuum than the one we inhabited. Page after page reeking with innocence and vulnerability, though we were aware of neither at the time. A too much younger version of myself stares back at me. I look into his eyes, trying to find some evidence of who I am now. I wish he could see me.

"Is that you?"

The voice came from directly behind me and scared the shit out of me. I turned to see to whom it belonged. It was a woman of indeterminate age, looking a little experienced for forties or well preserved for sixties. Attractive and easy smile, unlike most of the ones on the pages before me. She reached her arm over my shoulder and pointed her finger at my grade-nine photograph.

"Yes and no," I said.

"I know what you mean. You're Professor Pepperfield, are you not?"

She came around from behind the bench as she posed the question. I looked hard at her, feeling I should recognize her.

"My granddaughter was in your English class not long ago. She pointed you out to me one day when we were walking downtown. Her name is Niamh MacAmhaloibh—she was particularly impressed on the first day of classes when you called out her name with the correct pronunciation. You were the only one of her professors to do that."

I remembered the student, mostly because of her unusual Irish name, but also because of her copper red hair and freckles. I remembered that she, like her grandmother, seemed to be of indeterminate age.

"She was a good student," I said.

"You were a good teacher. She was quite taken with you. She had never heard of E.E. Cummings before your class. She hasn't forgotten him since. I've become quite a fan myself."

"I'm glad to hear that."

"I don't suppose you remember me, though?"

I looked at her face again, leaning my head away from her as if the added distance would trigger my memory. Her hair, like her granddaughter's, was red, though not so coppery, perhaps because older.

"You have me at a disadvantage," I admitted reluctantly.

"We were in the same Shakespeare class in third year. With professor Corlawney—remember him?"

I did remember him, but I still could not remember her.

"I remember you," she continued, "because of that time we were studying *The Tempest* and we had watched the 1960 George Shaefer film version and you argued that Jane Fonda would have made a better Miranda than Lee Remick because her voice had the perfect combination of confidence and vulnerability. Do you remember that?"

I remembered being smitten with Jane Fonda—I still am, and I do remember that I was as seduced by her voice as I was by her physical beauty. It was a true voice.

"Professor Corlawney then said, 'Mr. Pepperfield, are you planning on being a film director in the near future?' I'm sure he meant it as a slight on you, and your very red face showed that you took it in that way, as well. He said 'Mr. Pepperfield' in his best stentorian voice. That's why I remember you. Long time ago, eh?"

"What did you do with your degree?"

"I put it in a frame, left it with my parents for safekeeping, and went backpacking around Europe. I started in England, crossed the channel, headed south through France, Italy, and on to Greece, circled back through every other country in Europe and finished in Ireland. That's where I met this wonderful Irish man who was just about to emigrate to Canada, so I took him home with me."

"I love Ireland."

"You've been there, then. What's your favourite part of Ireland?"

"Well, I've only been there in the pages of books, and even then I've only been to once place: Connemara. There was a wonderfully obscure book I picked up in an old used bookstore somewhere—I can't remember where—Ethel Mannin's *Connemara Journal*."

I can't remember where, nor can I remember what drew my hand to it on the shelf. It was one of those book-hunting days when one hunts without a prey in mind. How I came to find myself in the section of Irish history, I don't know; perhaps I was on my way from the fiction section to the poetry section and lost my way. The volume is a slim green one and I had to get my eyes right up close to the spine to read the title. Perhaps it was the ghost of Ethel Mannin herself who recognized in me a sympathetic reader. Truth be told, I was more taken with Ethel Mannin than I was with Connemara of the 1940s, which she wrote about, in much the same way that I was more taken with Jane Fonda than I was with *The Tempest*. There was something about Ethel Mannin's voice on the page that attracted me.

"You're not one for the beaten track. Niamh liked that."

"Teaching in the same university where I got my undergraduate degree would suggest otherwise."

I had never been off the continent, had never travelled to places outside my head. Many of the students I taught had had a wider experience of life, though it was not always clear to me that they were able to navigate their own minds. It was supposed to be my job to make sure they were supplied with the appropriate charts and compasses and intersections of latitude and longitude, and once they were all seated in their various boats with their life jackets on, I was supposed to give them the oars so that they could propel themselves, but too many of them weren't interested in rowing; too many of them, when they did ply the oars, got caught up in the physical details of movement and paid no attention to where they were going.

"What did Niamh do with her degree?"

"Same thing I did with mine, though she still hasn't come back yet."

To go away and never return. I knew only the negative image of that; I left myself decades ago and have not yet returned to who I am. I trekked stubborn through the seasons of my life without myself. Now I wanted to get back, but I didn't know how.

"When you came back here after backpacking around Europe, did you feel that you were coming back to a place you knew?"

"I knew it still, but I'm not sure that it recognized me. We had to create a new relationship."

"And your Irish husband, has he ever returned to Ireland?"

"We go back every couple of years."

"Is the Ireland he left still the same one he visits when he goes back?"

"For him, I think it is. There's a part of him he never brought with him here to Canada."

"Is he sad about that?"

"He talks about a kind of melancholy that is 'mottled with peacefulness.'"

"I think I understand that."

I understood melancholy and mottled, but I couldn't truly say that the peacefulness part was there for me. Even the melancholy and mottled, though, was something I could apply to these past decades of my life only in the immediacy of retrospect that was a consequence of my recent retirement. To live inside melancholy mottled with peacefulness sounded like a kind of treasure you find in your back yard without even looking for it. How much treasure is lying at our feet and we just don't notice it for what it is? Here was this woman, a former classmate and the grandmother of a former student of mine—we had come this far in the conversation, and I had wandered down various side streets of its main thoroughfare—and I had not yet asked her what her name was.

"What's your name?"

"Harriet. I used to be Harriet Leonard."

The name did not ring a bell, but that might be because the bell had long ago lost its tongue.

"It's nice to finally meet you, Harriet Leonard."

She parted from me more gently than she had introduced herself, and I was left once again with my lapful of yearbooks. Rather than search out the progressive stages of my adolescent aging through the photographs of five successive yearbooks, I instead focused my attention on those aforementioned photographs of students surreptitiously caught in the act of everyday activities and the ones in which they mugged for the camera. I was in none of those photographs. Why were my everyday activities in the halls and rooms of my high school not worthy of the camera sleuths? Why was I not considered an appropriate subject for the camera that advertised itself in my presence? Because I was one of the "bright kids," and we seemed to inhabit not only the periphery of intelligence and good grades, but also the periphery of popularity. We did not hang out with the average kids, nor did we hang out with each other. We were the islands that defined the ocean. And, as I had just found out, even in university, attractive and intelligent young women like Harriet Leonard, while they may have noticed me, did not befriend me.

‡

I needed more coffee, even if it could not live up to the perked coffee I had shared with Deborah only a couple of hours ago. I wanted to find a comfortable café, but I didn't want to carry these hard-edged containers of nostalgia with me, so I deposited them in the nearest trashcan, with the understanding that if they were still there when I did decide to return home, I would withdraw my deposit.

I found a comfortable café and sat myself down in that altered state that takes hold of you when you haven't slept for over twenty-four hours. I was going to order just a coffee, but I decided I was still hungry and ordered a Reuben sandwich. As I was waiting for my meal to arrive, I was taken by a not unexpected sadness at having so summarily tossed my high school yearbooks into the trash. But with that pang of sadness came the inescapable fact that I was now clearly past middle age; what lay before me was a horizon cluttered with fragments of my past, populated with loss rather than possibility. The best I could hope for was to transform the mosaic of suffering and disappointment that was my past into a golden age that I could relive in moments of self-pity. Still, I was convinced that if I could get back to that place before school and religion bastardized my life, I could save myself without drowning in a tragically flawed nostalgia.

Three bites into my Reuben sandwich, I noticed how the sun was angling through the window across the aisle from my booth. There were some hanging plants in the window, which broke the fat ray of sunlight into warm wafers, some of which were scattered across my table. I was reminded of the Shattering of the Vessels Deborah had told me about and how it was our mission as humans to collect these sparks of divine light, to repair what is broken—*tikkun olam*. How does one pick up pieces of light? I was then reminded of the scene in *Franny and Zooey* where Franny and Lane are sitting in Sickler's restaurant and Franny is staring at a blotch of sunshine about the size of a poker chip on the table cloth, staring at it as if she wanted to lie down in it. The more I ate of my sandwich and fries and salad, with the pieces of sunlight now spattering my own body, the more I felt that I, too, would like to lie down in the light. I was tired.

The waitress wafted by and asked if my sandwich was satisfactory. I told her that it was the best of all possible sandwiches in this particular intersection of space and time; then asked her what her life was like in the same coordinates. Clearly, no one had ever presented her with such an observation and consequent question.

"Sometimes there are just no words," she said, as if caught in the spotlight after receiving an unexpected reward.

There was something about her voice and her smile that magnified the distance in years between us. I felt embarrassingly old. Why was that? When I was in class, facing dozens of eighteen to twenty-year-olds, I did not feel that distance of age as I did with this young waitress. True, I was too often frustrated by their lack of intellectual navigational skills, but that part of me that had remained twenty years old ever since I was twenty, obscured the actual number of years between our ages. Do I contradict myself? Very well then, I contradict myself; I am large, I contain multitudes: sixty-year-old selves, twenty-year-old selves, five-year-old selves. I pondered once again that five-year-old self sitting against the garage door, soaking the new warm sun into his morning-chilled body. I took my time to savour each mouthful of the rest of my sandwich, reminding myself that I had a plan.

‡

I walked back to my house to pack an overnight bag. On my way, I checked the trashcan where I had deposited my yearbooks. They were still there. I retrieved them, convincing myself that they and I deserved a better ritual of separation.

Back in my undergrad days, I took this train ride at least once a month, going back home with regularity for as long as I had a girlfriend I had left behind when I went off to university. This lasted well into the spring semester of the first year, at which point she left me behind. I had not ridden this train in decades. The house I grew up in was now the home of my older brother, who moved back into it once both our parents had passed. Jerry and I could never seem to find enough common ground, even as we got older and the search should have become easier, to encourage any kind of communication other than the perfunctory exchange of Christmas and birthday cards. I always made sure to send birthday cards to his wife, Silvia, and my nieces, Judy and Debby. I think that if it weren't for Jerry, I could have grown a substantial relationship with the three of them, and it often pained me that I could not be a better uncle to my nieces. They now had children of their own, but I had never met them and didn't know when their birthdays were. In spite of all this, I had decided I needed to go back and sit against the old garage door one more time, hopefully without any of them noticing me. If, as had been the case since both their daughters had gone off to university and moved out of home for good, Jerry and Silvia were taking their annual trip to Mexico for the month of September, the house would be empty.

For the train ride, which would take a couple of hours, I brought along Ethel Mannin's *Connemara Journal*, which I would pull off the bookshelf and read every few years. As always, when I read the book, passages that had reached out and grabbed some place deep inside me the first time would reach into that same place again, while passages that I couldn't remember being in the book before would suddenly choose to make themselves known to me.

Ethel Mannin wrote the book in 1947 when she was the same age as the century. She wrote about middle age and old age as if she didn't expect many more years in front of her, and I was surprised, in reading the book this time, to find how much she wrote about aging and death, but perhaps I wasn't able to notice it until now, when I could better recognize the subject. I suspect she had always been an old soul and she may have surprised herself to have lived to eighty-four. "But it is the one compensation—there are no more—of growing older," she wrote, "that we acquire at least the rudiments of wisdom." I hoped she was right about this. She also observed that "middle age is the time to stop gulping and sip, delicately, discriminatingly."

Middle age, it seems to me, is a relative term. Most often we apply it to that tipping point in our lives where ascendancy gives way to descent into old age and death. But that applies to the physical body more than it does to the mind—at least for those of us who do not succumb to dementia. I find that my mind, thus far, has been honing itself to a sharper and sharper point as my joints lose their elasticity and my flesh sags in places that make the image I see in the mirror less and less appealing. As for my spirit, well . . .

I look out the train window every now and then, hoping to recognize landmarks from long ago, but either I have misremembered them or, as is more likely the case, they have been transformed or have disappeared altogether. The only landmarks I can count on for persistence through time these days is books, especially the first editions I have collected over the years. I may read them differently each time I come back to them, as I must, but they do not change; it is I who changes. Ethel Mannin and my bespectacled former student of the previous evening would beg to differ with me. They assert that though we gather new knowledge and meet new people and develop more complicated and elaborate tastes as we grow older, we remain fundamentally the same person we were when we were six years old.

One landmark did remain on the other side of my train window. Horner Creek. I noticed it from the very first train ride I took between home and Riverdene. There was nothing unusual about Horner Creek—it ran through its own narrow valley, with high grasses and a few trees on either side. If it had been entered in an exhibition of creeks where viewers could explore each one for a mile in each direction and then pick their favourite, I don't think Horner Creek would ever have made the short list. But it had a quality of loneliness about it, perhaps for that very reason. It was an unassuming creek, a creek that did not try to attract attention to itself; a creek that, somewhere in its long ago past, had experienced a great sorrow that no other creek or person could understand. It comforted me to see it again.

☦

I got off the train at a much more cluttered station than the one I used to know, and walked a mile or so to a motel that I could use as home base. I had two orders of business, the first of which required me to walk another mile to Saint James church.

"I'd like to report a theft and a spiritual assault and battery that took place here about sixty years ago," I said to the priest who responded to my knock at the rectory door. Like all priests I had ever encountered, he was too old to ever have been young. In all the years I had grown up and gone to this church, I had never ventured around the back to the rectory. I couldn't imagine a priest not barricaded from his congregation behind the altar rail or in the mysterious fuzziness of the confessional, or standing in front of our class, scaring the shit out of us.

"Are you sure this is the right . . ." he began, with a confused look on his Catholic priest face.

"I'm sure," I cut him off.

"Come in," he said, knowing, in good conscience, that he couldn't turn me away.

He waved me into a chair in front of a desk and made his way to the opposite side and sat down.

"Now," he began, his elbows on the desk, fingers extended, pressed together just below his chin as if about to begin praying.

"Do you know what a *klipah* is?" I interrupted.

"A kleepa?"

"Yes, the Jews have it, but I'm wondering if you know of a Catholic version."

I proceeded to repeat Deborah's explanation, as best I could remember it.

"I suppose," he mused, after I had finished my explanation, "that you could be talking about the devil."

How uninspired, I thought. Everyone had devils. I wanted him to own this Jewish *klipah* in a Catholic priest sort of way. I then forwarded him my experience with the venial sin of merely thinking of a swear word and the consequent hell I lived in for weeks afterward.

"You—and by 'you' I mean you as a representative of the Catholic Church—stole my pure and unsullied consciousness, then you sent your Catholic version of a *klipah* to live in my head to assault and batter my spirit forever more."

I waited for him to propose some sort of compensation package, but he was obviously floundering in foreign territory. Whatever words he was searching for were not to be found in the Catholic priest's guide of the perplexed.

"At least admit," I said, "that you fart and that your shit smells. Can we begin with that?"

He looked frightened, the poor bastard. This pleased me greatly, though I wasn't sure that this counted as compensation.

"I suggest you say ten Our Fathers and five Hail Marys," I offered, as I rose from my chair and walked out of the rectory. I hoped that I had scattered his defences well enough that some *klipah* found a way to take up residence in his Catholic priest head, though I'm sure he had a much stronger *klipah* than even I had. Perhaps, if nothing else, I had made him a good candidate for exorcism.

As good as this counterpunch to the Catholic gut felt, I kept going back to Deborah's sense of God and faith. Perhaps Jews didn't eat their young the way Catholics did, or perhaps Deborah somehow escaped the slaughter either through serendipity or through her own intuitive sense of herself and of the world. Whatever it was she had, I wanted to have it, too. Yes, I had been robbed and beaten when I was too young to defend myself, but at some point someone should have explained to me that there was more than one way to define salvation and there was more than one way to get there.

‡

Afternoon was aspiring to evening as I walked down the long road from the highway to the house I had grown up in. My house—I still call it that, though there is nothing about it that is mine anymore—still stood on the corner of two lazy curving roads, one of them eventually looping back along the shore of the lake. The houses I remembered on either side and across the road had been replaced by shiny soulless mansions that had metastasized throughout the neighbourhood since I had last been here. I walked slowly around the corner of the yard, carefully checking out the windows to make sure that Jerry and Silvia had, indeed, vacated it for the month. It looked as if they had, which was good news for me.

From there I made my way towards the old Ramswood Estate, weaving through its vast acres of woods, which were now not quite so vast, due to a large portion of them having since been subdivided. The old woodland paths that were once maintained as such by the regular tramping of children's feet—no adults ever wandered through these woods—were now boardwalks. No more squelching of bare feet in the muddy spring ground, no more catching burrs in your socks on hot summer days. Another theft from my childhood to report, but to whom?

I felt the particular absence of the old Ramswood mansion. Colonel Ramswood died when I was about five years old, so for me the mansion was a kind of ghost house that I knew only from the outside. The boy I was imagined what the rooms looked like, how high the ceilings were, where the fireplaces were in each room, which grand ladies had danced with which great men in the ballroom, which servants dreamed, as I did, of owning such a house to live in. It was difficult now to know exactly where it stood, pocked as the pristine landscape of my boyhood was with houses.

I remembered my way to the marsh and to Garter Snake Hill, which is the only name I've ever known for it. In all my time growing up and exploring the woods and the marsh and the hill, I had never seen a garter snake anywhere on it. Maybe there used to be hordes of garter snakes, but some Saint Patrick-like figure had long ago banished them. Or maybe one of my ancestor kids saw a lone garter snake on the hill one day, told his friends, and next thing you know, everyone was calling it Garter Snake Hill. I paused by one of the "new" explanatory signs, about six feet by four feet, that had a map on it. On the map, Garter Snake Hill was called The Knoll. There was a mother and her son, who was about seven or eight years old, standing there reading the sign. I said, "You know, I grew up here. When I was a kid we always called this Garter Snake Hill." The mother tried her best to pretend I wasn't there; the boy looked towards me as I spoke, but he paid about as much attention to what I said as he would have to someone speaking in a foreign language. He wasn't at all interested in the fact that I had grown up there or that kids had a different name for that hill that only other kids knew. He was a kid, too, but he just didn't care.

As the marsh itself was untouched, so too was the shingle bar, a rare geographical formation that separated the marsh from the lake. At certain times of the year, usually spring and fall when the weather roiled the lake, a narrow passage determined itself through the shingle so that the waters of the lake would slosh into the marsh.

I sat down on the flat grey shingle stones and stared out across the lake for a while, then turned and stared across the marsh into the tall bulrushes and the farther woods that were still left. It was here that I had taken my first kiss; I say taken because when Mary and I kissed, it was as if we took the gentle energy of woods and water and sky that cupped us in its hands and stained our lips with it so that they would recognize each other in a kind of profound intimacy that is available only to the innocence of youth.

The sun disappeared behind the trees on the far side of the marsh, which was a signal for me to find my way back to the motel and some takeout food for dinner. As the several landmarks along the train route were mostly gone or transformed, so, too, were the landmarks of my home village. With equal measures of faith and hope I walked back to the highway, then west looking for the Saturn Drive-In, which used to have the best hamburgers in the world. It was still there, though the best hamburgers in the world were not. I was too tired and hungry to take my order back to the motel, so I slumped myself into a booth and as I munched my way through a disappointing relic of my past, I thought of Mary. I wondered where her life had taken her after we each went off to different universities. While she lived at home and went to university in the city, I chose a university over a hundred miles away, and we never saw each other again. It makes no sense to me how that could have happened, how we became suddenly invisible to each other like that. She was my first girlfriend, and the details concerning why we stopped being boyfriend and girlfriend were somewhat fuzzy. Something about her mother not wanting Mary to settle for a neighbourhood kid when there was a whole world of eligible young men waiting to challenge each other for her hand once she was older and more mature. For some reason, her mother didn't think much of my prospects. Her mother, like mine, had probably since shuffled off her mortal coil, which, I imagined, lay in the dark corner of a museum of mortal coils in a town that had been left behind when a new highway was built to bypass it. In my sleep-deprived state, this speculative piece of information seemed like a logical reason to assume that it was now safe to talk to Mary again, if I could only find her.

One of the things that had not changed about the Saturn Drive-In was the public phone at the end of the counter, complete with a phone book. Since Mary was most likely married with a new last name, I looked up her brother. Maybe he was still in the area. He was. After an awkward phone call during which I remembered myself to him as best I could and we traded abridged *Readers Digest* versions of our lives, he told me that Mary was living not far from their original house. He gave me her address and phone number, and off I went, an ornery hamburger elbowing its way through my digestive tract. I wondered if it might not be too late to call, but such concerns of social etiquette were no longer functioning in the sleep-deprived state I was in.

Mary's married house was on the other side of the marsh from where we grew up. She answered the door.

"Oh my god! Levi?"

"Yes, it's oh-my-god-Levi. How are you, Mary? How have you been?"

The fact that we recognized each other after so many decades was comforting. It's fascinating to me that, in situations like this one, we can still see the fifteen-year-old person lurking inside the old skin that, no matter how old and floppy it becomes, will never be able to hide that fifteen-year-old from someone who knows where to look. We hugged each other in a formal kid of way and she invited me in, where we sat facing each other from either end of the sofa in her living room. We attempted to fill in the wide gap between where we had once been and where we were now, but quickly came to the conclusion that there was probably a better way to navigate ourselves across that expanse. We set out for the marsh—she, an apparently happily married woman with three grown children and four grandchildren, who had retired as a nurse five years ago, about to take a night time walk with a dear childhood friend; I, a man who had never really known what women wanted or needed, who had retired only months ago, about to take a night time walk with the woman he had always believed was the one who got away—a man with fanciful ideas about where this walk might lead them, encouraged by her putting her arm through his as they walked.

"I always thought you would make a good father. It's too bad you never had kids."

I should have disabused her of that flawed perspective, but I was flattered, nonetheless, so I said something platitudinous like "my students were my children." We followed a dirt path that wound through the woods, parallel to the creek.

"Do you know the Many Worlds Interpretation of Quantum Mechanics?" I asked.

I was not good at segues.

"All possible alternatives to any situation are real," she said. "A single photon, when fired at a card with two slits in it, will go through both slits at the same time. Something like that."

"For every alternative we choose, we choose them all, but can only be conscious of one of them."

"We exist in several worlds at the same time—is that what you mean?" Mary asked.

"Perhaps," I said, "we'll meet other versions of ourselves on this walk. I feel as if some of my best versions are still haunting these woods."

They were certainly still haunting me.

"Are your parents still alive?" I asked, trying to shift myself on to safer ground.

"Both gone. Within months of each other. Dad went first and I think mom couldn't figure out how to live without him."

"Do you think they loved each other?"

"In their own ways. Not ways I'd choose, but theirs was a different generation, growing up in the Depression years. Your parents?"

"Both gone, too. I don't think they loved each other. I think they knew within weeks of their marriage that they'd made a disastrous mistake, but given the time and the culture and the fact that they were Catholic, well, they just stuck it out until it killed them."

When you walk out of evening into night, the darkness becomes its own light. Garter Snake Hill rose before us like a voice made of silence, which only those who come upon it in the night can hear. We walked inside that voice until we came down the other side and then down on to the shingle bar. I remembered the very spot I had kissed her too many years ago. I wondered if the stones and the trees and the water remembered us, if they held our imprint.

"Do you miss who you used to be?" I asked her.

"I never really had time to think about it."

"But if you think about it now?"

"I have fond memories."

"It's okay if you don't want to talk about them."

"I'm happily married, Levi."

But she didn't take her arm out of mine.

"Sorry, my versions of myself sometimes get confused. It must be the spirit of the marsh."

We sat down on a log and looked out across the water. Off to our left the lights of Toronto defined the curve of the lake. The water shushed the shingle like the slow breath of time that never stopped, no matter how much you tried to weigh it down with memory.

"It's different when you go away and come back," I said. "I suppose you never leave anything behind if you never go away."

"I didn't get left behind, Levi. We're still friends, I hope."

We were never just friends. She was the girl next door; I was the boy next door. We were destined for beauty or sadness. There were no other options. It pained me that she didn't seem to understand that, or that she had forgotten that. It made me sad to know that I was going to lose her again tonight.

We walked back the way we came. It was the far side of midnight when I said goodbye to her on her doorstep. She kissed me on the cheek and squeezed my hand. I turned and walked back to the marsh, alone.

‡

Wallowing in the darkness of the dead of night is always a more rewarding enterprise than wallowing in the light of day, even if you burrow into the pile of clothes lying on the floor in your closet and close your eyes. I was back on the shingle bar listening to time breathe. I wished I could breathe like that. Like Buddhist monks in the bamboo groves of Thailand, separating themselves from this world, denying all the alternatives except for one. My one alternative right now was the purity of sadness that had become its own entity, divorced from cause.

I paced the darkness out of the shingle bar, the hollow clink of my steps perforating the perfectly regular shush of water, the moon like a ghostly galleon tossed upon cloudy seas. I listened to the stones for secret messages. I tried to walk the innocence of the five-year-old boy back into my body, hoping it would rise through my feet, up my legs, through my gut, into my heart, thence to flood my brain. I tried to walk backwards through time to find Mary and never leave her. Then I just walked, back and forth, measuring the length of the shingle bar in time and space. I walked until the sun turned everything pink and it was time to find my garage door.

The driveway was still the same gravel driveway it was when I was a kid. As it crunched under my shoes with each deliberate step I took, I was immediately transported into a past whose residue caught in my throat. I sat down and leaned against the garage door and waited. I realized now that I was asking this imminent moment to accept a piercing light of expectation that would most likely shatter it. I could not back out now; there was no other future moment of my life that could substitute for the one in front of me. I thought I should have better prepared myself, but I knew that if I had tried to do that, I would have analyzed myself out of this quest; I would have turned down the call to adventure. Spontaneity, I tried to remind myself, was my elixir and I had drunk it down.

There it was, a flaming orange swelling coming out of the trees. I closed my eyes. The insides of my eyelids began to glow a sympathetic orange, the sudden heat shivering my body. I sucked in my breath, but then forgot how to let it out. Panic surged through every part of my being. I hoped I was dying; I was nothing but the flesh and bones of pure loss. But my five-year-old self was in distress and I needed to give him emergency heart-to-heart resuscitation. I forced my eyes open, arching my back against the garage door. The perfect orange ball of the sun had floated itself free of the treetops. I expelled the air that had taken my body hostage and then started gulping in new air as fast as I could, grasping at words—a world of made is not a world of born, a made of world is not a born of world, a made of born is not a spirit of made, a spirit of world is not a yes by made, world by born is not an if by yes, when by spirit, if by yes, yes by when, spirit by if . . ."

"What're you doing?"

The tiny voice sliced into my ear like a blade of broken light. It came from a boy standing about three feet to my right.

"Who are you?" he asked.

"What?"

"Who are you?" he repeated.

"Who are you?" I countered.

"I'm Bobby. I live over there," he said, twisting the top half of his body towards a mansion across the road where the modest bungalow of old Mr. and Mrs. Bigelow used to be. "You don't live here. Why are you here?"

"Because by if, if by . . . it's okay, someone I know used to live here."

"Who?"

"Me."

"Where do you live now?"

"Far away from here."

"Why are you here?"

"I'm just visiting."

"Were you waiting for the sun?" he asked.

"Yes, I was."

"I do that, too. I close my eyes like you did"—how long had he been watching me?—"but I don't do that other part you did when you opened your eyes. Are you a crazy person?"

"No, I just got a little afraid for a moment."

"Afraid of what?"

"The sun, maybe."

"I'm not afraid of the sun. I like it."

"That's good."

"It makes me warm and it makes everything bright. I'm not afraid of anything."

"You're lucky."

He looked at me, confused. He couldn't see the connection. This was a boy without a *klipah*. I wanted to warn him about the *klipah*, but I knew he wouldn't understand what the hell I was talking about. It was the same disconnect that I felt when I was teaching—how could I expect eighteen-year-old students to understand a poem written by a fifty-year-old poet who was writing from a life experience that these students simply didn't have? Each new academic year I would choose pieces that spoke to me, that I figured my students must be exposed to if they were going to be fully functioning human beings, but they were pieces that spoke to me because I was of a certain age, because I could finally recognize what the writers were trying to tell me, because those writers were me. But my students were not of that certain age, and whatever they were going to learn about being human would have to be from their own limited perspective. Of course, to them, it was not limited at all; to them, my perspective was a frumpy one, and the fact that I would even use a word like "frumpy" proved just how frumpy I was.

"I have to go now," said the boy.

Of course, he did. Why would he want to spend time with a crazy old man?

"Have a wonderful day," I said to his back as he was walking away. He turned to look at me with that same confused look on his face. What other kind of day was there?

I stayed there, propped up against the garage door, trying to make sense of anything. I went back to my thoughts about teaching poems to eighteen-year-old students written by fifty-year-old poets. Perhaps I should have given them a diet of Keats, who died when he was twenty-five—could I have convinced them that "heard melodies are sweet, but those unheard are sweeter"— could I have enticed them into the unknown by that route? Or a diet of Rimbaud who, though he died at thirty-seven, stopped writing when he was twenty-one, which, for him, turned out to be middle age: "I am the saint at prayer . . . I am the scholar of the dark armchair . . . I am the pedestrian of the highroad by way of the dwarf woods . . . I might well be the child abandoned on the jetty on its way to the high seas . . . The paths are rough."

Yes, the paths are rough. Sometimes there is not enough light; sometimes the light shines too intensely. What I had come back for, I couldn't retrieve. It was a book that had been discontinued, then remaindered, then removed from the shelves altogether.

‡

Back in Riverdene by noon, I did not feel like the hero who has answered the call to adventure, who has found the boon he was seeking and returned to share it with the community, thus becoming master of the two worlds. I wasn't quite certain what the boon was that I had set out to find, but I knew that I had not found it, and whatever community existed here was not my community. The world here, which I had left when I set out, and the world I had travelled to and returned from—I was master of neither of them.

Part Two

Do you think of me as often as I think of you?
 —*Richard Brautigan*

I RETURNED TO a Riverdene of steady rain, the thick grey sky low enough that I could almost reach up and touch it. I imagined that it would feel like poking a bowl of Jell-o, though I wasn't sure what flavour grey Jell-o would be. Perhaps a soft shivery flavour that would make your tongue feel as if it had gone somewhere it had never gone before and was excited to be there. When I got to my house, I stood on the steps leading to the porch and the front door and let myself be soaked to the skin. People walked by and looked at me the way the little boy had looked at me by the garage door. I eventually went inside, removed my clothes, like peeling an overripe mango, took a hot shower, re-clothed myself in the warm dry vestments of a retired professor, fed myself a very late breakfast of bacon and eggs, perked myself a pot of coffee, and sat on the swing chair on the porch, watching and listening to the rain. About a half hour into the program, I was lured back into the house by a ringing phone.

"Hello?"

No answer.

"Hello?"

Still no answer. I hung up the phone and went back out on the porch. About an hour later, now thoroughly hypnotized by the steady fall of rain, I was interrupted again, but this time by a voice coming from the bottom step of the porch.

"Professor Pepperfield?"

She spoke my name as if trying to confirm that I was who she thought I was.

"Violet?"

I spoke her name in the same way.

"I hope you don't mind me showing up at your house like this."

"Please, come up out of the rain."

I shifted to one end of the swing chair and motioned her to the other end.

"Was that you who phoned me and hung up without speaking?"

"I just wanted to make sure you were home."

"Would you like some coffee?"

"Sure. If you don't mind."

I went back into the house to get some fresh coffee, wondering, on my errand, how to respond to this very unexpected visit. Back on the swing chair, I waited for her to open the proceedings.

"I wanted to give you a second chance," she said. "After the other night."

She took a sip of her coffee.

"I've never tasted coffee like this before."

"It's perked."

"Oh yeah, I recognize it now. My grandmother has perked coffee."

"So, a second chance."

"The possibility of redemption. Like in Eliot."

"Oh?"

> "'Love is most nearly itself
> When here and now cease to matter.
> Old men ought to be explorers
> Here and there does not matter
> We must be still and still moving
> Into another intensity
> For a further union, a deeper communion.'"

"You've been reading the Quartets."

"You inspired me."

"You see me as an old man," I said, rather than asked. I wasn't going to touch the first two lines about love.

"As an explorer," she said.

> "'We shall not cease from exploration
> And the end of all our exploring
> Will be to arrive where we started
> And know the place for the first time.'

"That's sort of what I meant that night when I said that we never lose anything. Even if what we never lose is just the desire to keep exploring."

She paused long enough to raise her cup to her lips, but hesitated before they made contact. She lowered the cup an inch or two from her mouth.

"At the bar . . . you were hurtful. I didn't expect that from you."

"I'm sorry."

And I was. I had to admit that I often thought of Violet. I missed her—I began missing her as soon as that class was over. I missed how, during that semester, she slowly became beautiful because of her mind. I was hurtful towards her at the bar because I think, in that perversely constructed desire peculiar to the male mind, I wanted her to heal me. Now, here she was, hoping to redeem me.

"Can I tell you something?" she asked.

I could sense danger.

"Sure."

"There's another reason I like Eliot. I like the kind of Christian he is."

"And what kind of Christian is that?"

"A poetic Christian. A Christian who understands metaphor. Don't worry; I've done my research. I know about how and why he wrote 'The Waste Land' and 'The Hollow Men,' about the nihilism of the post-World War One period; I know about his family's roots in Boston Unitarianism and how when he went to Europe he did a kind of reverse cultural journey, choosing the traditional European culture over the new world American culture."

"'We need to know how to see the world as the Christian Fathers saw it; and the purpose of reascending to origins is that we should be able to return, with greater spiritual knowledge, to our own situation. We need to recover the sense of religious fear, so that it may be overcome by religious hope.'"

"Exactly. That's from his *Idea of a Christian Society*, right?"

"Right."

"For me, it's not just Eliot, though. I'd like to choose Christianity the way Franny Glass tried to."

"You mean the Jesus prayer?"

"Maybe. But it was the book the prayer was in—*The Way of a Pilgrim*. She was trying to explore, the way the pilgrim did. I want to explore like that."

"There are a lot of other roads besides Christianity to choose from."

"You can only choose one at a time. Franny knew that. That's why she couldn't explore the Jesus prayer and be with Lane Coutell at the same time and stay sane."

She looked at me over the top of her cup, then shifted her gaze to the rain falling beyond the shelter of the porch.

"Salinger never wrote about Franny again?" she asked of the rain and of me.

"Rumour has it that he wrote more stories about the Glass family and that they'll be released sometime after 2015. Same thing with Holden Caulfield."

"That sounds exciting."

"Maybe, but there's a danger, too. The first stories were so good and there's been so much time—decades—since they were first released that any follow-up will have a hard time meeting the pent-up expectations that the readers have. The same kind of thing happens with music. I have always lost interest in my favourite musicians after about their third or fourth albums—James Taylor, Neil Young, Led Zeppelin, Yes. But I've never been able to find any new and upcoming musicians who make me feel what I felt with my originals. Maybe it says more about me than about them. Although with James Taylor"—I could feel myself beginning to ramble as if I'd lost the reins to the horse I was riding—"I find that even though I don't think he writes songs that are as good as those first ones, I'm still attracted to his voice. He could sing any old thing and I'd listen to it just because of the quality of his voice. His voice—that's never changed."

I forced my cup of coffee to my lips to give myself a chance to stand back and observe the minor revelation I had just stumbled upon. Perhaps I was stumbling into redemption. Or perhaps I was simply so sleep deprived I had stumbled into an alternate universe. One inhabited by the unintentionally seductive Violet. She, too, recognized the moment and let it breathe. She smiled.

"One thing about the Jesus prayer, though," I said. "How does one know if Jesus hears it?"

We settled ourselves back into the rain-adorned silence, each of us suddenly realizing how close together we were sitting on the swing chair.

"I like you again," she said. "Do you like yourself again?"

"What do you mean?"

"That night when you made me walk out on you—c'mon, surely you didn't like yourself after that."

"You're right; I didn't. I'm sorry."

"You already said you were sorry. Once is good enough for me."

She smiled over the edge of her cup of coffee. She tipped the last swallow of it into her mouth.

"That was good coffee. Thanks."

She got up to go.

"Want me to put this in the sink?" she asked, waving the empty cup towards me.

"It's okay. You can just put it on the railing."

"I'm glad you're back," she said. "See you around."

Back where, I wondered.

‡

"Wanna tell me about it?" asked Deborah as we exhaled smoke from our cigarettes.

The "it," to which she referred, was not my swing chair meeting with Violet. That was territory best left off our map for now. Instead, I explained, as best I could, how my quest to find my five-year-old self had failed.

"Of course it did," she said, as if it should have been as obvious to me as it was to her.

"Your sixty-year-old self setting out in search of your five-year-old self by taking a train to get there is like the guy wandering around his house looking for his glasses when they're on top of his head the whole time."

"I thought the association of place with feeling would uncover something."

"Get rid of your *klipah*, you mean?"

"Something like that."

"I've got another way to put this, if you're interested."

"I am."

"Stop renting your life. Why don't you just move in and take possession once and for all? Put your own furniture in it—take time to choose some art you like, chairs and tables whose wood invites your eye and your hand, a comfortable bed—big enough to allow for a passenger on trips to oblivion. And by the way, when I talk about oblivion, I'm not just using a throwaway word. In the Jewish mystical tradition oblivion has to do with *Ein Sof*, that mystery of absolute nothingness. *Ein Sof* is a kind of oblivion; it's a place of forgetting. You forget what you think you know or what you think you should know. When you're in that place you're perfectly nowhere else because there is nowhere else."

She exhaled the last of her cigarette.

"When's the last time you slept?"

"I can't remember."

"Most men fall asleep after a round of sex. You haven't slept for days; I've given you the most passionate parts and behaviour of my physical body—twice—and still you don't sleep. I must not be doing it right."

"Oh, you're doing it right."

"Then why don't you fall asleep?"

"I'm in limbo. It's a Catholic thing."
"How do we get you out of there?"
"You help me pick out some furniture."
"You trust me to do that?"
"I just stole your cherry; it's the least I can do."
"You're so romantic."
"You're so ironic."
"You love that about me."

It was the first time that word had appeared in any of our conversations where we were the subject of those conversations. We both felt it elbow every other word around it into the ditch. I wasn't sure that I'd ever truly been in love with a woman. Aside from projecting my own anima onto various women at various stages in my life, I knew I had also experienced lust and infatuation, but love was like a Platonic essence that I wasn't sure could ever be experienced for what it truly was, even though, at the same time, I believed that I would one day find it. I didn't know how it would happen, but I trusted that I would recognize it when it did. I thought it would be like a light switch being flicked on in a dark room—sudden and unmistakably illuminating.

"Should we go back to our corners and take the eight count?" proposed Deborah.

"Let's go out for something to eat and a walk," I suggested.

We chose the local burger shop, which had the best, and messiest to eat, chili dogs. It was difficult not to wear as much of your meal as you ate, but, more importantly, it didn't allow for conversation without spitting food on each other.

Meal accomplished, we each went to our respective washrooms to clean up and then went walking. It was a wordless walk for the first many minutes. Deborah took my hand, as if she always did that when we walked together. She had never done that when we walked together.

"We could just recognize it for what it is," she said.

"What is it?"

"Oh, damn this to hell!"

Her hand that was holding my hand pulled me up and we stood there facing each other.

"It's Rosh Hashanah, the new year, the beginning of ten days aimed at Yom Kippur, the Day of Atonement, and I'm either going to repent for what I have not done up until now or for what I'm about to do. 'Who shall rest and who shall wander, who shall be at peace and who shall be tormented, who shall be poor and who shall be rich, who shall be humbled and who shall be exalted?' So here it is: It's love, Levi. It's always been love, at least from my side of things. Can you recognize that?"

"Can you recognize something you've never seen before?"

"You've never been in love with anyone before?"

"If I had been, wouldn't I still be with that person now?"

"Are you that naïve, or are you being wilfully stupid? Have you never read *Cyrano de Bergerac, Great Expectations, Twelfth Night*? Have you never read the poetry of Emily Dickinson or Edna Saint Vincent Millay?"

I had, of course, and as various of the plots and poems flashed through my mind, I realized, finally, that I had been in love with Mary. That revelation immediately spawned a second one—Mary had always existed for me as a possibility, slim though it might have been, but in closing the door to that possibility once and for all, she had forced it to migrate somewhere else. It now joined forces with the possibility that had been Deborah for fifteen years. If I said yes to Deborah, there would be no more possibility in that area. Did I really want to live the rest of my life without the possibility of possibility?

"I feel as if I just bit into the apple," I said.

"I've been holding it out to you for a long time."

"Is there any way this story can end well? It didn't seem to the first time."

"Every story in the world depends on that story. Without that story, you couldn't be a professor of literature. Without that story, I couldn't be a rabbi. Eating the apple brought uncertainty into this particular world. That's what makes us human—how we deal with uncertainty. But the world of certainty still exists, too; it never disappeared. We just lost consciousness of it. The point is, we're in this story—this one right here, right now. This story where I just admitted my love for you. This story that now depends on what you're willing to admit."

"So, the pen is in my hand."

"It is. And I know you well enough to know that you like to write alone. But I want you to read me what you end up with. See you later."

Deborah squeezed my hand and walked back the way we had come, trailing her long September shadow behind her like a wake.

‡

I didn't want to go back to my place, so I started walking for the sake of walking. I didn't want to name what it was Deborah and I felt about each other; how it was we behaved with each other. I was comfortable with adjectives, but I didn't want to be handcuffed by a noun. I had lived inside two nouns for most of my life: student and teacher; they had defined me into a kind of stasis that rendered all the verbs of my way of being in the world ornamental rather than productive. Now I had some more context-specific nouns to wear: predicament, dilemma, conundrum. I just needed to find the right verb to resolve these nouns. What writer could come to my rescue? Whitman? Too broad, too everyman. Thoreau? Not when the relationship between a man and a woman was concerned. Plath? Not unless I wanted to end up with my head in the oven. Eliot? Too intellectual. Brautigan? Too Brautigan. Rilke? Too much sadness, beautiful though it was. Cummings? My favourite of his poems relied on "is," which was no more than an equal sign between nouns and adjectives: "love is more thicker than forget," "it is most madly and moonly," "it is most sane and sunly."

When, after some long while—minutes? an hour?—I focused myself on my immediate surroundings, I found that I was at the gate of the university. Again. Why did I always end up here? I went in to the diner and sat down in an empty booth.

"Coffee, neat, with a side of cinnamon toast, dear?"

I don't recall ever being in the diner when she was not working. I also don't recall ever knowing her name.

"What's your name? I've been coming in here forever and I don't know your name."

"Luella."

"That's the perfect name."

"It's always worked for me, dear."

She smiled and made her way down the aisle back towards the kitchen. From the opposite direction, the front door, came Violet.

"I'm not stalking you, I promise," she said. "I come here all the time. Anyway, I'll leave you alone."

She walked down the aisle and then back again. Towards the front of the diner, then back again.

"There aren't any open booths. Could I sit with you?"

"Why not?"

"Well, I guess that's what I'm asking you. If this is too uncomfortable, I can leave."

"Please," I said, motioning to the bench on the other side of my table.

"Have you ordered?"

"I have. The cinnamon toast is really good here."

"I know. The best comfort food ever."

Ah yes, comfort. I could have used some when I sat down in my empty booth. If not comfort, at least some measure of spiritual stillness in which decisions that needed to be made could be encouraged to appear without being wrenched from the reluctant cosmos, like a tooth being pulled without anaesthetic. The unfortunately serendipitous appearance of Violet was not, however, the kind of help I was looking for.

"I'm just going to use the washroom," said Violet. "Could you order me a club sandwich if she comes back before I do?"

I placed Violet's order as Luella placed my cinnamon toast and coffee on the table before me.

"So, what have you been doing since last time I saw you?" I asked when Violet returned.

This was meant to be mildly humorous, a kind of salve to soothe the awkwardness of a second meeting so soon after the first one only a few hours before, but my delivery left much to be desired.

"I went home and masturbated."

I coughed my mouthful of cinnamon toast into my coffee, which splashed on to the table where Violet's hand was resting. She calmly picked up a napkin and wiped her hand clean. She smiled.

"Just wanted to see a side of you I hadn't seen before. Wanted to see if that side was operative."

"Jesus!" I coughed out a bit more of my toast.

"Where?"

Violet spun around, her eyes searching the diner, then she turned back to me with a decidedly mischievous look on her face.

"Should I apologize?" she asked.

I was still trying to regulate the functioning of my upper esophagus and bronchial passages as her club sandwich arrived.

"You okay, dear?" asked Luella.

"Fine," I rasped.

"Let me freshen that cup of coffee," she said, picking up the cup with bits of partially chewed toast floating in it.

"Anyway," Violet continued, "you asked me what I did and I told you."

I was not used to being in such an uncomfortably disadvantageous position with a student, even though technically, she was no longer my student. Still, the transition was a rude one. I was desperate to re-establish some sense of my intellectual acumen. Perhaps Violet mistook my look of concentration. Perhaps not.

"You're trying to picture me masturbating, aren't you?"

"No! God, no!"

Now I was. I slid to the aisle end of the booth.

"I have to go to the washroom."

"Are you going to . . ."

"I'm just going to the washroom."

I closed the door behind me and leaned against it. If dialogue was a teeter-totter, she had just jumped hard on her end and catapulted me into the wide-open air and a rude crash landing. I closed the lid on the toilet and sat down on it. Poetry could not save me now. There was only one line of defence left. I stood up, took a deep breath, walked to the sink, splashed some cold water on my face, and opened the door.

"So," I said as I slid back into the booth, "were you lying down or just sitting in a chair? Standing up, maybe?"

"What?"

"When you were masturbating. Did you just shove your hand into your jeans or did you slide them down to your knees? Maybe you stripped naked. If I'm going to picture you masturbating, some details would really help."

"Touché."

"So, Christianity. I pictured you more as the Buddhist type."

"There's no god in Buddhism. I need a god of some sort."

"Just one?"

"I figured I'd start simple."

"Thus, Eliot?"

"You pointed me down that road."

"It's a good road, as far as pure poetry goes."

"Pure poetry?"

"Where truth and beauty don't need props."

"I'll have to think about that. It's a big idea."

"Would you like some homework?"

"I'd love it."

"First Corinthians chapter fourteen. An ostensibly Christian text, but you can easily dig below that surface. See what truth and beauty you can find there."

"When is this assignment due?"

"A week?"

"Written or oral?"

"Both."

"They make a good club sandwich here," said Violet, redirecting her attention from the intellectually to the gustatorially edifying.

‡

Back on home ground, I perked a pot of coffee and sat my very tired self down on the porch, again. The last time I had gone three nights in a row without sleep was when I was finishing my second attempt at my doctoral dissertation. My first attempt was "From Whitman to Brautigan: The Turning of the American Kaleidoscope." I kept turning that kaleidoscope and turning that kaleidoscope, pointing it at Whitman and Frost and Sandburg and Eliot and Cummings and Ginsberg and Brautigan, and I couldn't stop turning it. I couldn't focus it anywhere without feeling that I was leaving something out—there was so much I was leaving out. I had to make choices, but the possible perspectives were endless. I resolved to keep Whitman and Cummings and Brautigan and jettison everyone else. Then I tossed Cummings overboard and was left with Whitman and Brautigan—two American literary freaks. From "Song of Myself" and "I Sing the Body Electric" to "The Pill Versus the Springhill Mine Disaster" and "Rommel Drives on Deep into Egypt," I exploded my being across the pages of words, shrapnel flying everywhere.

I chose for the epigraph to my dissertation a poem by Brautigan:

> Adrenalin Mother,
> with your dress of comets
> and shoes of swift bird wings
> and shadow of jumping fish,
> thank you for touching,
> understanding and loving my life.
> Without you, I am dead.

I was warned against my choice of writers by the senior, soon-to-retire Americanist in the department: "Whitman was an arrogant, infantile, sententious, solipsistic fantasist, and Brautigan is a dysfunctional drunkard and unlikely to achieve even Whitman's dismal level." What he would have said if I were writing my dissertation several years down the road after Brautigan had shot off the side of his head with a gun would, no doubt, have added to his stature as a pronouncer of literary merit in those circles where the members assumed that one's behaviour off the page was the only useful determinant of what was left behind on the page.

"Who do you think was, or is, the more essentially American man of his time—Whitman or Brautigan?" was the question one of the dissertation committee members tossed at me.

It was a loaded question, and I knew it. At the very outset of the project, I was warned that Richard Brautigan was not substantial enough for a doctoral dissertation, especially if I was planning to focus on his poetry. If I were to suggest that Brautigan was the essential American man of his time, I would set myself up for the conventional attacks of over-the-hill conventional academics on the sixties as a cultural ephemeron. I was also sure that no one on the committee had ever played with a kaleidoscope.

"That's not a choice I need to make," I answered.

"Make one, since you didn't do it in your dissertation."

"There is no choice to be made," I said. "They're both in the kaleidoscope. That's why I chose that image. The writings of both men are true. The writings of both men are beautiful."

"Truth and beauty, Mr. Pepperfield?"

It was more a derisive statement than a question. I waited him out.

"Truth and beauty? Could you find two more abstract nouns in all of literary criticism?"

Still a derisive statement rather than a question. I continued to wait.

These were men who were caught between the traditional forms of literary criticism, which weren't all that far removed from reliance on such aesthetic attributes as truth and beauty, and the incipient onslaught of a more cold and calculated approach to literary criticism, which, as universities began to shift from liberal arts institutions to corporate-driven job-training centers, felt the need to make the humanities more scientific.

"Pray, Mr. Pepperfield, give us your working definitions of those terms."

"They both depend on context, of course, as all abstract terms do. Truth, in the context of both Whitman's and

Brautigan's work, is the courage to not be deflected from the ability to observe without censorship. It is Whitman's unflinching intention to shine a light on every blade of grass, on every human pursuit, on every human connection; it is Brautigan's surrender to perception altered by the uncensored imagination. No truth is absolute except in its particular application in a particular circumstance, like flint and steel producing a spark that begins a fire. The spark and the fire are the beauty. That beauty can warm us on a cold night or burn down our houses when we forget to pay attention."

"But still," the committee member persisted by retreating to his previous point, "you would be inclined to stop the turning of the kaleidoscope at some point."

"I wrote this dissertation the way Whitman and Brautigan wrote their poetry. If I were to write this dissertation again next year, it would not be the same as it is today. One never puts down the kaleidoscope," I said, "until one is dead."

The committee turned down my dissertation but grudgingly admitted that I had an intellect they thought was worth giving a second chance. "Come back in one year with a proper dissertation," they instructed me. "And please use secondary sources this time." And so, I did, with a dissertation on T.S. Eliot: *Eliot's Four Quartets Through Four Lenses*. I read "Burnt Norton" through the lens of Saint Augustine's *Confessions*, "East Coker" through the lens of Ecclesiastes, "Dry Salvages" through the lens of the *Bhagavad Gita*, and "Little Gidding" through the lens of Julian of Norwich's *Revelations of Divine Love*.

Though I had a year to complete it, I didn't really get a handle on it until the last three months, during which time I got less and less sleep, until, as I said, I went three nights in a row without any sleep at all heading into my defence, this time successfully. Then I slept for two days. After the first night, my roommate kept tiptoeing into my bedroom every couple of hours, holding a mirror to my mouth to see if I was still alive. When I did wake up, I realized, in the aftermath of the intense process of writing my dissertation, that I was standing outside myself and that I couldn't get back in. The image of the kaleidoscope had begun as a benign one, but had somehow worked like a stroboscope used on a person already under the influence of a hallucinogen. The effects, I feared, were permanent. Something happened, though, when I got in front of a classroom full of students. In the same way that I had learned to project my anima onto unsuspecting women, I learned, as a teacher, to project my self who was standing outside myself on to my students, thus leaving me with the delusion that I was making a true and beautiful connection, at least for the first few years. Thus resulted the great paradox: using literature, which had forced me to stand outside myself, to get me back inside myself. How many times had I begun the semester by explaining to my students that poetic language is paradoxical? Language puts an artificial element between us and our environment—it separates us from our environment. We put the word "tree" between us and the actual tree. Then we use poetry to break down that barrier. All this time I had been using literature as a means to find out who I was, when it was literature that kept taking me out of who I was.

Now, as I was re-experiencing several nights in a row without sleep, a fierce light was shining on this paradox—that was the noun that trumped predicament or dilemma or conundrum. That was the right word, the true word because it couldn't and didn't need to be resolved. The word that contained the beauty of the incomprehensibility of being. This was what Whitman was talking about when he said,

> 'Out of the dimness opposite equals advance,
> always substance and increase, always sex,
> Always a knit of identity, always distinction,
> always a breed of life.
> To elaborate is no avail, learn'd and unlearn'd
> feel that it is so.'

That's what Brautigan meant when he said,

> 'There are comets
> that flash through

our mouths wearing
　　　the grace
　　　of oceans and galaxies.
　　　God knows,
　　　we try to do the best
　　　we can.'

If I went to sleep now, in what condition would I wake? Would I wake up whole or more fractured? Would I open my eyes and say "I am that I am," or would I be finally mute?

Part Three

*There is that in me—I do not know what it is—but
I know it is in me.
Wrench'd and sweaty—calm and cool then my body
becomes, I sleep—I sleep long.*

—*Walt Whitman*

I ROLLED OVER on to my back, my arms flung out on either side of me, and let my eyes fall open. I tried to get my bearings, but got stuck for a disconcerting time in the transition between worlds. How long had I been . . .

"He had his piano lesson right after mine every Monday afternoon."

Trisha Brewster?

"I sat across the aisle from him in grade nine homeroom."

Evelyn Gardner?

"Our piano teacher was a nun. We had our lessons in the convent by the school. We were in grade five. I'd walk out of the piano room and he would be sitting there on the bench. I'd look at him and smile. He would look as uncomfortable as a boy could be."

"We'd get to our desks first thing in the morning, waiting for our teacher to tell us to settle down for the morning announcements over the loudspeaker. Same thing, though—I'd sometimes smile at him and he'd just get all flustered."

"We didn't go to the same school," said Trisha. "He had no idea how shy I was, how much courage it took for me to smile at him, and how defeated I felt every time he didn't smile back."

"I liked him," said Evelyn. "I wanted him to speak to me, maybe even to walk to classes together."

"He doesn't even remember us now."

"I do! I do remember you—both of you."

"He hasn't thought about us in all that time since those days."

"Maybe not, but I liked both of you. I just didn't know how to . . ."

"He didn't know how to deal with those constant erections he came to school with," said Evelyn. "He wasn't the only one, of course—all the boys had them, but he thought he was the only one. He really believed he was desperately detached from the world around him."

"Poor thing, he couldn't find his voice. And even if he did, he had no idea what words to sound with it."

"What are you doing here?" I pleaded. "What time is it?"

"To think of time…" said a male voice. It belonged to an old man with long white hair and a long white beard. He was leaning on a cane.

"So many trout, so little time," said a second male voice belonging to a middle-aged man with long dirty blonde hair and a drooping moustache. He had a fishing pole in one hand, a revolver in the other.

"Why don't you gentleman go downstairs and put the coffee percolator on?" suggested Trisha.

"I have wounded men to attend to," said the first male voice, tugging sadly at his beard.

"I'm going fishing," said the second male voice.

The gentlemen turned and left, as if they had not come together.

"I know those men," I said, trying to lift my head from the pillow.

"So he thinks," said Trisha.

"He spends too much time thinking," said Evelyn.

"He's very good at it. Too good at it."

"We all do what we're good at, I suppose. What did you end up doing?" Evelyn asked Trisha.

"I'm a concert pianist. You?"

"A professional escort. I own my own business now."

"If he came to you now, would you 'escort' him?"

"I would. I'd get two school desks like the ones we had in homeroom. I'd place them in the middle of the room side by side, just as we used to sit across from each other and I'd offer him a glass of champagne. I'd honour his uncontrollable erection."

"Perhaps I could play some Schumann in the background. What do you think he'd do?"

"Search for the appropriate line of poetry to hide behind."

‡

I rolled over on to my stomach and buried my face in the pillow. I felt like a frog splayed on a dissecting table. I flipped myself over again, staring at the ceiling, no scalpels in sight. Just voices.

"He looks tortured," said a female voice to my left.

"What's he got to feel tortured about?" said a male voice to my right.

"The only torture you recognize is your own," she said.

"I have you to thank for that," he said.

"Mom? Dad?"

"Is that why you fucked Sybil Passmore every Saturday night when you said you were out playing poker with 'the boys'? Yes, I knew about that."

"Mary's mother?!" I yelled, completely offended. "You were fucking Mary's mother?!"

"Ever since we had him," my father nodded in my direction, "you didn't want to do it anymore. I had to get it somewhere."

"Mary's mother?!"

"You were never there for him. He had to spend his whole time growing up on his own."

"What about you? I was working all day. You could have done something with him. Don't lay all that torture stuff on me."

"I wanted to buy him that set of encyclopedias. You said we couldn't afford it."

"We couldn't."

"But you could afford a new car."

"*We* could afford a new car. The car was for the family."

"And for Sybil Passmore. *We* never went anywhere in it."

"You never wanted to go anywhere."

"You never made any plans."

"It takes two."

"You and Sybil Passmore."

"What about Trixie Belden's mother? Did you fuck Helen Belden, too?" I sputtered.

"Give it a rest."

"You didn't. You could have at least found someone I didn't know; that he didn't know," said my mother, nodding her head towards me.

"The kid made something of himself. What does it matter?"

"He's sleeping with a woman rabbi and letting himself be seduced by a Jesus freak at the same time, and you ask 'what does it matter'?"

"That's what poetry types do. What's the big deal?"

"Do you know that I used to read poetry to him every night after he fell asleep? After you were shagged out and were snoring into my face, I'd get out of bed and tiptoe into his room and read him poetry. I loved poetry when I was in school. You didn't know that about me, did you?"

"You never told me."

"You should have been able to figure it out. I read him my favourite poetry by Emily Bronte. I bet you didn't know that Emily Bronte wrote poetry."

"'I'll walk where my own nature would be leading:
It vexes me to choose another guide:
Where the grey flocks in ferny glens are feeding;
Where the wild wind blows on the mountain side.'

"—oh my god, that's Emily Bronte! You read that to me?" I cried.

"Does it really matter that Emily Bronte wrote poetry?" my father asked.

"Poetry matters."

"So does fishing. I took the kid fishing."

"Once, when he was five years old."

"I rented a rowboat down at the mouth of the river. Bought a pail of minnows. Gave the kid one of my old rods. Baited the hook for him. Showed him how to watch the float—if the float got tugged under the water, he had a hit. Well, he got a hit even before I did. I helped him reel it in—a two-pound trout. Damn fine fish. Showed him how to take the hook out of its mouth. There he was, sitting in the boat holding his very first catch in his hands. He looked up at me like he wanted to ask me something, but he didn't say anything. Then he threw the fish back in the water. Then he asks me, 'Do you think it will be okay? We didn't kill it, did we?' That's why there wasn't a second time."

"Did you even try to explain to him what fishing was about?"

"What fishing was about? Jesus, anybody knows what fishing is about."

"He was five years old."

"I was five years old," I repeated, for emphasis.

"Everybody was five years old," said my father. "We grow up. Everybody grows up."

‡

The rain. I could hear the rain pattering on the roof. I've always loved the rain. The rain is the world telling everything else to be quiet; telling everybody to just listen. I'm standing by the creek in the woods near Garter Snake Hill. The rain is prickling the surface of the creek, playing a harmony over the slow rippling ostinato of the current. There's no one else around; there's probably no one else anywhere in the world. Just me and the woods and the creek and the rain.

"What's the fishing like here?"

Just me and the woods and the creek and the rain and this familiar guy with long blonde hair, a drooping moustache, and a floppy felt hat I notice standing next to me. He's got a fly-fishing rod on one shoulder and a creel slung over the other.

"Just suckers," I said. "They run up out of the lake, through the marsh, and into the creek, usually around Easter time. When I was a kid we used to make spears out of broom handles or the old shafts of hockey sticks. We'd stick a long nail in one end."

"Good eating?"

"We just killed them. We kept count to see who got the most."

"You like that sort of thing?"

"I hated it. I hated it then and I hate it now when I remember it. I did it because all the other boys did it. I was trying to fit in."

"Did it work?"

"Not really."

"No trout here?"

"No trout."

"Too bad."

"I liked that poem about the trout-coloured wind."

"Yes, the fish music."

"I liked the store that sold trout streams in various lengths."

"Everybody should have their own trout stream. It's important to have someplace to fish, to learn how to measure out your line, to inscribe the sky before letting it drift down on to the surface of the water."

"They said you weren't that good a fisherman."

"Depends what you're fishing for," he said.

"I like the rain," I said, tilting my head back and catching the drops on my tongue. "Rain music."

"That's good music, too."

"I liked all the women on the covers of your books."

"They're fine women, aren't they? They're back in the truck, waiting for me. I just wanted to check out this creek."

"Back in your truck? All of them?"

"Sure."

"Do you know about the Many Worlds Interpretation of Quantum Mechanics?"

"No. I just know about fishing and women."

"And writing."

"Same thing. I'm going back to the truck now. You should get some sleep—you look tired."

"I am tired."

"By the way," he said as he began to walk back down the creek, "that hill over there. Swarming with garter snakes. Never seen anything like it."

"Say hello to Beverly and Victoria and Valerie and Hilda and Michaela and Marcia and Shiina," I yelled out to his disappearing back.

"Say hello to Deborah and Violet and Mary," he called out over his shoulder.

The rain prickling the surface of the creek, playing a harmony over the slow rippling ostinato of the current. Just me and the woods and the creek and the rain.

‡

"I wouldn't have said it quite that way."

He was sitting on the end of the bed, his long white hair and beard hiding much of his face. But those eyes; there was no mistaking those eyes.

"Said what?" I asked.

"The women at the speed dating table—you said, 'I fart and my shit smells.'"

"Surely you of all poets would understand the honesty behind those words. I didn't shrink from the raw unadorned truth. You never shrank from the truth."

"Truth and beauty—isn't that what you espouse?

> 'Welcome is every organ and attribute of me,
> and of any man hearty and clean,
> Not an inch nor a particle of an inch is vile,
> and none shall be less familiar than the rest.'

"You're fond of quoting; you should have opened with those lines of mine, instead."

"I needed to use my own words."

"But where was the poetry? I listened to you define truth and beauty to those literary bumps on logs—a kind of restrained yawp, but a yawp, nevertheless. What do you think a poet is?"

"You said the great poet is the equable man, the arbiter of the diverse. You said the greatest poet hardly knows . . ."

"Yes, yes, I know what I said. I ask you what you say. Do not filter yourself through my words."

"A poet is someone who sees all of life as a poem."

"What is a poem?"

"It's what exists when we focus our attention on it."

"What have you been focusing your attention on?"

"Teaching."

"What did you teach?"

"Literature. Ideas. Ways of perceiving things. I taught you."

"I didn't even teach me. I was just the finger pointing at the moon. Go out and look at the moon, man!"

"It's raining."

"So?"

He swept his hand across the space between us and the ceiling. When his hand had accomplished its wide arc, there was a dark purple sky perforated with stars, his aged finger pointing up at a full yellow-white moon hanging in the midst of them all, overwhelming them all. There were blue-grey veins in it, like an eye that has been staring too long without blinking. It pinned me to the bed. I tried to move my arms and legs, but couldn't. I was soaked with rain.

"Would you like me to write a letter home for you? I've done that for many a wounded and dying soldier."

"A letter home?"

"Just tell me who to address it to."

"I'm not a wounded and dying soldier."

"Oh, but you are. You said so yourself: 'Levi Pepperfield, recently retired professor of English, walking wounded.'"

"I received a knife wound to my arm, but I'm not dying from it."

"Then you're dying from your wounds as a recently retired professor of English."

"That's just a metaphor."

"You want truth and beauty, but you want it without metaphors?"

"You never used metaphors."

"Just the one."

I looked back up at the moon. Already it had drifted ever so slightly westward from where it was just a few minutes ago. I didn't want it to move; I wanted to stare it into place until I was done with it. I never wanted to be done with it.

"I want a cup of coffee that lasts forever. Hot perked coffee that never cools down, in a cup that never empties."

"That's what all the wounded and dying soldiers ask for. They all miss forever."

‡

"Why do you think he should write a letter to me?"

I turned my head, which weighed more than all the dreams that never come true in the history of all five-year-old boys, and aimed it at the woman's voice. She had brown hair and brown eyes. She was tall. Her intonation was marbled with hope and uncertainty.

The old man had removed himself to the corner of the room, sitting on a chair reading *The Pill Versus the Springhill Mine Disaster*, smiling and nodding his head. He looked up at the young woman standing at the foot of my bed.

"A man who is wounded but doesn't believe he is," he said, "needs to write to a woman who is wounded and knows she is."

"I'm probably too wounded for him."

"You want to be healed?" the old poet asked.

"I want possibility."

"So does this man."

"Just because I want possibility doesn't mean I'm wounded," I said.

"Would you write to me?" she asked me.

Hope struggled towards confidence, uncertainty shifted towards vulnerability, not just in her voice, but in her posture. I had a sudden urge to reach out my hand to her, but I didn't.

"Yes," I said.

She smiled, first at me, then at the old poet.

"You recognize her, don't you?" he asked me.

"Esther Greenwood?"

She was back to her skinny as a boy and barely rippled look after shedding the weight she had put on because of the insulin injections in the asylum.

"Yes," she said.

"From *The Bell Jar*," added the old poet. "You've taught that book, have you not?"

"Yes," I said.

"And you've always wanted to meet her. So," he said, taking a notebook from his inside jacket pocket, along with a pencil, the end of which he touched to his tongue as he flipped to an open page, "what would you like me to write to her?"

I sat up in my bed, leaning my overweight head against the wall.

"Is any of this real?" I asked.

"All I know is that it's true," answered Esther. "So please, write me a letter."

She reached her hand out to me, knowing she was too far away for me to be able to touch it, then let it drop back to her side. She turned and left the room.

"Ready now?" asked the great poet.

"You really think I should write this letter?"

"That's what I'm here for."

I stared into his watery blue eyes to see if he was humouring me, but the playful light shining from them was sincere. What the hell, I thought.

"Dear Esther," I began. "I suffered with you when you were overwhelmed with possibilities, when you were imprisoned by them, when you believed you had lost them all. You were imprisoned by everything around you, by all the expectations you couldn't distinguish as your own or others'. I wanted to free you. But I realize that, in the end, I want to imprison you for myself. To me, you're the 'still unravished bride of quietness' on Keats's Grecian urn. I also realize, though, that you imprison me, though it is not your intention to do so. This, I think, is how desire, maybe even love, must work. This is the true nature of sacrifice. Truth and beauty depend on the transcendence of time and space, of what we call reality. I, like you, according to the wise, white-bearded poet, am a wounded and dying soldier who struggles for transcendence but cannot achieve it. Whatever the case, I've always wanted to meet you, so let this letter be an opening to that continued possibility."

"I'll make sure she gets this," said my scribe, folding the letter and putting it in the inside pocket of his jacket.

He rose from the chair with the help of his cane, made a tip of the hat gesture, and left the room.

‡

I felt as if I'd been lying on the bottom of the ocean for days; the weight of water, like the weight of dreams, heavy but translucent. My clothes clung to my skin, but from salt water, rainwater, or simple sweat? Somehow, I had floated to the surface of days and nights; somehow, I was able to sit up, to swing my legs over the side of the bed, and reorient myself to the life I had left behind, how long ago was it? How many days and nights? I rubbed my hand against my stubbly whiskered chin.

I clomped down the stairs and into the kitchen to make a pot of coffee. Steaming mug in hand, I directed my feet towards the porch, picking up the mail strewn across the floor by the door on the way. Nothing of interest there, except a letter, the handwritten address seducing my eye with its fluid curves of fountain pen ink. I took it out to the porch along with my coffee.

Two or three glorious sips into my coffee, I opened the letter.

Dear Levi,

Thank you for your letter. Thank you for keeping your promise. You know, of course, that I love words as much as you do, but I also love the physical object of the letter itself—words that I can hold on to and they won't fly away. I will admit, too, that the cursive of your amanuensis gave your words a force equal to their content. I understand only too well the paradox of eternity and time standing still in Keats' poem—I wonder, are they the same thing? Is heaven, or whatever its substitute might be, allergic to time? Did Keats anticipate his own removal from time long before most would have thought it appropriate? I'm thinking of "Ode to a Nightingale." Anyway, I'm not even sure if all these questions are related to one another, and I'm sometimes afraid to pursue them for fear of relapsing into my craziness. I was crazy, you know. I often think of myself as a Roman candle exploding across the night sky—I try to follow every one of the coloured stars at the same time. So, let me try to pick just one and see where on the ground it lands, because I choose to believe that they all do land on the ground rather than disappear in the air. They lie in the dark like secrets hardly anybody knows about. Perhaps you would like to go on a Roman candle star hunt with me one day.

But to get back to just one of those stars—and each one has a different secret meaning—for this letter, I choose the wounded and dying soldier in the struggle for transcendence. You want us to live on the Grecian urn, but you fear that I might be La Belle Dame sans Merci—perhaps you're getting your Keats mixed up, or maybe I am. Nevertheless, let us add death to eternity and time standing still and see what we can make of this trinity—three consubstantial concepts in one. Perhaps you have been wounded by desire and you are dying into transcendence of that delicious demon rather than of time and space. Perhaps you don't want to transcend desire; perhaps you have been wounded, but you don't want to be healed. Perhaps you are dying, but you don't want to die. What is the word for this? Conundrum? Predicament? Dilemma? Paradox? Whatever it is, I will try to understand it without losing myself in it. Maybe you can do the same.

Yours in transit,
Esther

I went back upstairs to check my bed and see if I was still sleeping. Or dead.

Part Four

*We stopped at perfect days
and got out of the car.*
—Richard Brautigan

Esther and I were sitting on a bench on a tree-lined street as if it were the most natural place for us both to be.

"I brought you a present," she said. "It's a book of letters—Ovid's *Heroides and Amores*. Well the *Heroides* are letters—I thought that was only appropriate; the *Amores* are love poems. I couldn't find the letters in their own edition without the poems. Anyway, they're in Latin and English. I've always thought I should know Latin—it's another one of those possibilities that haunts me."

It was a red hardcover 1947 Loeb Classical Library edition. It felt good in the hand.

"Where are we?" I asked.

"In a book. Where else could we meet? Where else do people live?"

"Are we in *The Bell Jar*?"

"No."

"Then who's writing this story?"

"Someone we've both surrendered ourselves to."

"Who?"

"That's all I know. Writers find us, they observe us, they turn us into words as accurately as they can. Our own words, they keep; the rest they have to choose themselves. Some of them are better at it than others. They're like Plato's *daemons*—intermediaries between the gods and humans. The gods live forever and don't experience passion, whereas we humans are mortal and very passionate. *Daemons* are immortal *and* passionate.

Writers are passionate and like to *think* they're immortal, which is why they sometimes mess things up."

"So, we're the humans."

"We're the humans."

"And we're mortal."

"We're alive as long as people keep reading us."

"And if they don't read us anymore?"

"Then we don't exist anymore."

"We die?"

"We transfigure."

"We transfigure?"

"I haven't got it all figured out yet. I was hoping you might be able to help me with that."

Esther leaned back on the bench and aimed her face, which was soft and smiling, skywards. She seemed so much better, so much more relaxed than she was in *The Bell Jar*. She reached her arms out as if she were catching something falling out of the sky. When she caught whatever it was, she looped her arm through mine and pulled me up from the bench. I was a moderately tall man, but she matched me, inch for inch.

"There's a wonderful little shop a couple of streets from here that serves perfect hot apple cider. You can treat me."

To see her real smile, with all its nuances, on her real face with its real brown eyes, lit from somewhere deep inside the imagination of her being was so much more satisfying, psychically and viscerally, than just reading it in a book, with her on the inside of the page and me on the outside of it.

"What is our relationship in this book?" I asked.

"To be determined."

Should I tell her that I fart and my shit smells? Esther waved her arm that wasn't looped through mine at three women who were walking on the far side of the street in the opposite direction. They looked as if they were new to the town.

"Who are they?" I asked.

"Anna and Emma and Dorothea. They're here because of you, or someone like you. I'm not sure yet."

‡

I began to think, walking arm in arm with Esther, that I was living inside one of those fragments of light Deborah talked about. I thought that they might not be what she thought they were—they weren't fragments of a shattered world that needed to be reconstructed; they were individual worlds in themselves. Or maybe they were both—some version of the many worlds.

Esther was still twenty, but I wondered how old I was here—there were no mirrors in which I could check myself out, and when I looked at all the parts of my body I could see, it was like looking at a cloud on a windy day and trying to make it stay put. I'm pretty sure, though, that we're not vampires, but then, I think there might be some kind of transfusion of blood that happens not with teeth and veins, but with words and eyes. How did I get here? Maybe something to do with doors that open where you didn't know there were doors—wasn't that Joseph Campbell?

There were no internet cafés here; no people walking around pressing cell phones to the side of their heads; nobody wearing pre-torn and pre-faded jeans; no cars older than a 1954 two-tone Chevy. There is a measure of comfort in the absence of certain things. This place—it's not quite a city—perhaps a town that was only a village not so long ago—bleeds autumn from every tree. I never knew blood could be so beautiful; I never knew death was so alive. The butterfly is the truth of the caterpillar.

"What's that?" Esther asked.

"The butterfly is the truth of the caterpillar."

"I like that."

Another truth, I thought, was that even the most beautiful butterflies live for less than a year. This reminded me of my conversation with Violet, and with the woman at table number three, about how my favourite songwriters lose their ability to connect with me after their first couple of albums. It's the same thing with any powerful and profound presentation of an idea that says something to us for the very first time or shines a light on an unformed idea we've always had, but lights up every facet of it from every direction. Once something is illuminated perfectly for the first time, any further elaboration or explanation can only diminish it until it is corrupted beyond reclamation. Every creation story from every culture is like that; every religious revelation is like that—Judaism, Christianity, Islam, Buddhism, Hinduism—none of them is as pure and simple now as they were meant to be. The first album was all we needed—the beautiful ephemeral butterfly.

What if relationships between people were like that, too? Between lovers, between parents and children, between teachers and students? First contact is glorious, uplifting, inspirational, evocative, provocative. But then the lover becomes possessive, the parent becomes tyrannical, the teacher becomes loquacious. True revelation is desire bounded by the beauty of limitation. If I could understand that only now, at my age, how could my students have possibly understood it?

Our walk finally deposited us at the shop that served perfect hot apple cider.

"They're not as muddled as you think they are."

Esther began the conversation as if we were already in the middle of it. She cupped her hands around her mug of hot apple cider, elbows on the table, back straight, as one would sit at a lecture desk.

"Your students. You think they don't know as much as you do; you think they're not as wise as you are—and believe me, I thought my professors sucked up all the wisdom in the room, but I think now that wisdom is not dependent on age, and even age is a relative term."

She raised her hot apple cider to her lips using both hands, took a slow sip, and lowered the mug, but not all the way down to the table top.

"Think about it," she continued. "You believe your students are all so helplessly disoriented, yet here you are with me. I'm one of them. Do you think I'm helplessly disoriented?"

"You're not one of my students."

"Not one of yours, but a student, nonetheless. All of us are standing before that green fig tree with those fat purple figs hanging from every branch. We want to pick and eat every one of them, but as soon as we choose one, we lose all the rest. We're not disoriented; we're just overwhelmed by possibility. You, of all people, should understand that. You should understand that the curse of having to choose is never lifted. We all end up choosing one fig and losing all the others. You want to go back to that time when all the choices are still possible. Me, I'm in that time, afraid to reach out my hand to the fig tree. Do you have a cigarette?"

"I don't smoke."

"Liar."

"I don't smoke in these kinds of situations. Anyway, how do you know when I smoke?"

"That's how things work here. I didn't know I knew that until I said it. Would you like to make this a cigarette-appropriate situation?"

"You don't really want me to answer that question."

"No, I don't."

"Don't try to predict what you think I want. I just want you to be you."

"Said the physicist who thought he could observe the experiment without affecting it. Anyway, we're not as muddled as you think we are. You just have to get to know us. You used your students as the wrong kind of sounding boards; you used them as an *abat-voix*, a parabolic reflector that amplified the sound of your voice coming from the pulpit you spoke from, instead of as living, breathing humans who could hear your thoughts and send them back to you embellished with perspectives you couldn't find all on your own. Spontaneity is fine, but not every surprising idea is born inside your own head. You're not as alone as you think you are. Neither am I, for that matter. And you're not as alone as you want to be, which is a deliberate detachment from everything and everybody around you. And there's another paradox you like to live inside—desire and detachment. I know that because I recognize it. More than anything right now, you want to sleep with me. You want to save me from others and for yourself. More hot apple cider?"

Of course, I wanted to sleep with her—she was young and beautiful and intelligent and vulnerably wise, and no man, when he is not lying to himself, can resist such a combination.

"Notice how it's 1954 here? Think about it—and I promise I will do my best to not keep saying that—what happened to you that was so important in 1954?"

"I was five years old."

"And?"

"I started school."

"Anything special about that?"

Our second hot apple ciders arrived with a soft clunk on the table. Esther cupped her hands around this second one as she had the first one. She lifted it to her lips and blew across the top of it.

"I used to ride my bike to school. My mother thought I was too young and it was too far, but I insisted."

"And she let you. Why do you think she did that?"

"I never thought about it."

"So, anything happen on any of those rides to school?"

"I just rode to school."

"Don't you remember one particular day?"

"Remember what?"

"You were riding your bike from your house up to the highway and there's that hill that goes down to the creek, crosses it, and then goes up the hill on the other side. You were coasting full speed down that hill, and just as you crossed the bridge you heard someone call out your name and you turned your head for just a second to see who it was, but kept on riding. Remember that?"

"Vaguely."

"Weren't you curious to know who it was?"

"I guess not."

"You should have stopped. You should have stopped to see who it was."

"And if I had?"

"You would have lived a different life."

"Was it you who called out my name?"

"No. But I was there; we were all there."

"We?"

"It was a time when all of us were purely happy. For me, it lasted until I was nine; for you, I think it hardly lasted at all past that day. The point is, there were all these intersections of pure happiness; we just didn't know what they were back then. We didn't know what they were for."

"How do you know all this?"

"We all know all this, or at least knew it. We've just forgotten it. I remembered it. They tried to shock it out of me, but I remembered it. You can remember it, too."

"Just like that?"

"No, just like this," she said, reaching out her hand and putting it on mine.

"And this is?"

"Two blocks south and one block east of here there's a yard with a pile of leaves almost as tall as me. You should go jump in it. We can meet for dinner later, okay?"

Esther ordered another hot apple cider, pulled a copy of Aldous Huxley's *The Doors of Perception* from her coat pocket, and settled back in her chair to read.

‡

I felt as if I were on some drug trip of my own. My reducing valve had been rendered ineffective by Mind at Large. Both those terms were Huxley's, but I now understood them more clearly than ever before. I had dropped my fair share of acid in the day, but I was not as disciplined an explorer as was Huxley; I just wanted to get stoned. Good acid was wasted on me, as it was on just about everyone else of my generation. Timothy Leary had exhorted us to "turn on, tune in, and drop out," which sounded fuzzily rebellious, but we understood "turn on" to mean the unexamined decision to drop acid, rather than the examined intention to engage deeper levels of consciousness; "tune in" as not so much a harmonious connection to and interaction with our essential environment as a random turning of a radio dial; and "drop out" not as a conscious and determined search for self-identity and individuality as much as a stepping outside conventional behaviour for its own sake. We became addled rather than enlightened and we enjoyed it in the same way we enjoyed skipping classes, which is what we often did in order to drop acid.

"Are you new here, too?"

A gaunt man, a few inches taller than me, but reduced to my height by a stoop, which may have been the result of age—he was at least as old as me—or of the weight of the world as he understood it, put his hand on my elbow as he was passing me from the opposite direction.

"Yes, I just arrived," I said.

"Is this a good book to be in?"

"I'm not quite sure, yet. I'm here because I think I was invited in. Did you have an invitation?"

"I don't know, really. I'm not even sure that I'm really here. You see, I was sitting in my favourite chair—I use it only to read in—it's very comfortable—almost like a bed, except that you sit in it rather than lie in it—it rests my body so my mind can pay full attention to what I'm reading, but it doesn't rest it so much that I lose track of what I'm reading—you understand? Well, I was reading Herrick's Julia poems—you see, I have never been graced with a love that went in either direction, to or from me, and so I appreciate the fantasy of it—Herrick's Julia was born in the desire of his mind rather than existed in the reality of his world—he, like me, never married. Did I say that I was a professor of English literature? Specializing in seventeenth century poetry—Dryden, Crashaw, Marvell, Pope—I left Milton to the zealots—and, of course, Herrick. So you see, I was reading 'Julia's Petticoat' and was pondering the lines—

> 'Sometimes away 'twould wildly fling,
> Then to thy thighs so closely cling
> That some conceit did melt me down,
> As lovers fall into a swoon:
> And, all confus'd, I there did lie
> Drown'd in delights, but could not die,'

"—when I must have drifted into a kind of sleep, or perhaps it was that I did, indeed, die—are we dead?"

"I don't think so, but I'm not sure."

"Ah, well, yes. Anyway, I'm new here, wherever this is, and I wondered if you might be able to orient me."

"Given how this place seems to work, I'm thinking you must have been invited here by Julia. She should show herself to you soon; then . . . there's a woman standing on the corner," I said, interrupting myself in mid-sentence and nodding my head towards a very attractive woman in very old-fashioned clothes staring at us from the corner of the street.

She walked towards us, her flounce shivering the shape of her body like a willow shaping itself to a gentle breeze. She had a smile of recognition on her face.

"George," her liquid voice rolled over my companion like quicksilver, her gloved hand reaching towards his naked one.

"Julia?"

"Of course. I'm so glad you could come. I wouldn't have been able to make my way here if it were not for you. What year is it here? Never mind. You are an ardent reader—more ardent than analytical; you like to clothe your images with more than fabric, more than words. It is a disposition that draws the heart of me. And you," she said, turning her attention, blazing with full, cherry-ripe lips, towards me, "are a professor of English, as well."

Her eyes, her lips, her voice, her garment presented themselves as a delicately arranged bouquet of flowers, each individual colour and texture meant to create an is-ness beyond mere existence.

"Do we have the mark on our foreheads?" I asked.

"Yes, though not everyone can see it, and of those who can see it, not all can explain it. It goes directly from the eye to the heart, rather than from the eye to the brain. Also, Esther told me about you. By the way, she's expecting you at six at that bistro on the main street. And now, George," she said, blessing him again with her eyes, "let us stroll through the park until it's time to dine. Do you approve of this dress?" she asked him as they walked away from me. "I chose it . . ." but the rest of the sentence melted into the growing distance between us.

The streets that collected my footsteps were tinged with familiarity, in the sense that landscapes in dreams are familiar in and of themselves. The soft crunch of autumn leaves under my feet vibrated up through my legs and into my chest, such that each breath I took promised revelation. But they were revelations that refused to be burdened with any language dependent on the alphabet. Right now, however, I was in search of a certain pile of leaves.

The pile was as big and glorious as Esther had promised. I stood and looked at it, seized with a sudden but not altogether unexpected inhibition. Dare I, a sixty-something-year-old man, allow myself to jump into this pile of leaves? Of course, I still wasn't sure how old I was here in this place. I looked around to see if anyone was watching. Finding the coast clear, I ran towards the pile of leaves and jumped as high as I could into that mound of past possibilities. I landed in a crispy cloud with that earthy smell of everything that ever mattered and lay there, cushioned in possibility, staring up at the sky.

‡

"In this story," I said to Esther over the tops of our martini glasses, "we're nothing but words."

"Words are sparks; they set things on fire."

"So, your goal is to be an arsonist?"

"Arsonist, poet, neurotic. Whatever you want to call it, we need something to warm ourselves by."

"Would you prefer to be in a poem instead of in a book like the one we're in?"

"We can make it a poem."

"How?"

"Be the metaphor."

"Which is?"

"Take your choice. How about the labyrinth?"

"Are we trying to find our way in or our way out?"

"Doesn't matter, as long as you bring matches. So, where were you starting from when you became a teacher—were you outside the labyrinth or in the centre of it?"

"I never thought about it until now."

"Ah," said Esther, pushing herself back from the table, as if to get a better long view of the subject in front of her.

She pulled her martini, which was now at arm's length, towards her and stared at it as if she were trying to discover something about it.

"I think we move in both directions at the same time," she said. "Into the labyrinth and out of it. And at the same time, the labyrinth keeps moving and changing. Almost nobody knows that. But I knew it; at least I know it now. That's why I kept trying to kill myself—I was trying to make things stand still because that's what everybody said I had to do, but I couldn't keep still, not like they did. So, all I ended up doing was spinning on a fixed spot. And when they electroshocked me, when they gave me insulin injections, they just made me spin faster, like a spinning top, spinning in furious circles, but going nowhere. I was never crazy—not the way they understood crazy; I was just wounded, and they didn't have any bandages."

"Don't you wish you had a ball of red thread, like the one Ariadne gave to Theseus when he offered to go into the labyrinth and face the Minotaur?"

"As I said, bring matches. Sometimes you just have to set the labyrinth on fire."

‡

"I have some letters for you."

Esther handed me two envelopes with my name on them.

"Who knows I'm here?"

"They do," she said, pointing at the envelopes.

"How?"

"They needed to know where you were."

"But . . ."

"Just read them. I'll meet you for hot apple cider later.

I opened the first letter.

Dearest Levi,

For you are the dearest one to me, and with that I will desist from a further descent into the rococo of sentimentality. So, Esther Greenwood. How can you be wherever it is you are with her and not yet have figured out that I had been invited into the novel Now, Voyager *almost longer ago than I can remember? Why do you think I'm constantly watching the movie (even though the book is better, as they always are)? Do you not see the parallels in our lives, in the lives of Esther and Charlotte Vale? You do know that the title of the book is from a poem of Walt Whitman, do you not? 'The untold want by life and land ne'er granted, / Now voyager, sail thou forth to seek and find.' Of all the poetry of Whitman, which you so love, surely this should be your anthem. And surely you must know how it forever connects me to you. But, of course, you don't know any of this. Sometimes you frustrate the hell out of me.*

I was invited into the book by Charlotte Vale and by Tina Durrance, daughter of Jerry. Tina, of course, is Charlotte's younger self. Do you not get the similarity between those two women and you and your five-year-old self? Do you not get why Charlotte would invite me—a single, unmarried woman, a rabbi and counsellor, into the book? And have you figured out yet what happens to time when you're in your book with Esther? I could tell you, of course, but really, Levi, sometimes you have to figure these things out for yourself.

Here, I spend my time on Marlborough Street in 1930s Boston, where Charlotte Vale lives with Jerry's daughter, Tina, in one of those famous old brownstones that insist a human permanence into a changing landscape. I drove up to Vermont to see Cascade, both because it's so utterly beautiful up there, but also because I wanted to see how "nervous breakdowns" were dealt with before the profession of psychiatry became a dispensary for pharmaceuticals, or, in Esther's case, a descent into the psychic maelstrom of electroshock "therapy." There's a reason I became a counsellor rather than a psychiatrist. I have often wondered about relocating here permanently, but to choose to be immortal in an eternal present is not a decision to take lightly, as I'm sure you will find out, if you haven't figured it out already. First, I suppose, one must slough off all the doctrinal theories of the afterlife posited by the various religions humans have blessed themselves with since the beginning of time. I suppose I could get a job at Cascade, working with Dr. Jaquith. There are worse afterlives, I'm sure.

Anyway, I love you, my frustrating and frustrated Levi.
Love (and I mean it),
Deborah

I let the weight of the letter pull my hand down to my side where it hung like a flag waiting for a breeze to ripple it. I put the letter back in its envelope and opened the second one.

Professor Pepperfield,

This homework assignment has taken me farther afield than I expected, but then, maybe you knew that would happen. I seem to have been invited to first-century Corinth, the Pauline Epistles, though it took me a while to figure out how to navigate the passage—something like Jiminy Cricket wishing upon a star. It's all about faith, I guess.

I didn't actually get to meet Paul, but I did meet a very interesting woman who knows him well. You know how they say that behind every great man is a great woman; well, I suspect she's that woman. I'll try to keep you posted.

Yours,
Violet

Many worlds, indeed.
Esther took my arm. She looked up at me with sad curiosity.

‡

Meanwhile . . .

Part Five

Whoever you are, I fear you are walking the walks of dreams,
I fear these supposed realities are to melt from under your feet and hands.
—*Walt Whitman*

"I just want him to understand."

"Understand what?" asked Charlotte.

"That that female rabbi who just lost her virginity to him understands the balance between discipline and abandon, that both are true and beautiful, that one needs the other, that . . ."

"He needs you?"

"I just want him to recognize me—a female rabbi who just lost her virginity to a man whom she has desired for many years and who, through professorial absent-mindedness or simple emotional obtuseness, could not allow himself the same desire."

"You know, I've never lost my virginity, at least in that very physical and biological sense," said Charlotte.

"Do you want to?"

"I don't think I need to, now. There are many ways to complete yourself as a woman."

"I needed to lose that physical virginity."

"To figure out whether or not you were in love?"

"I already knew that."

"But it didn't feel like a complete love?"

"It felt like a one-sided love."

"And now that you're no longer a virgin?"

"I found out I like sex."

"What did he find out?"

"That he liked sex with me."

Charlotte reached across to the coffee table that separated her and Deborah. She picked up a silver cigarette case and opened it.

"Cigarette?" she offered to Deborah.

"Oh, what the hell," said Deborah, picking a cigarette out of the case.

Charlotte picked up the silver lighter and reached the flame across to Deborah's cigarette. She put the lighter back on the table and took a cigarette from the case for herself. Deborah picked up the lighter and lit Charlotte's cigarette. She tilted her head back and exhaled a long stream of smoke. Deborah did the same.

‡

"You are Violet? Welcome."

It was a bright and sunny afternoon on the edge of Corinth, the dark wind-sculpted water of the gulf to the north, the jagged-rocked Acrocorinth to the south. She was expecting to be greeted by Paul—that's who she thought had invited her here, on her own dogged insistence; she had an assignment to complete. The woman who stood before her was small but exuded a confidence, even power. Her voice had the same texture as the landscape and seascape—expansive, but detailed.

"Do you know Paul?" asked Violet.

"I know him well. I am Chloe. I helped him organize the church here. Would you like to walk with me?"

Chloe's sandaled feet clapped a muffled rhythm across the stone walkway, her eyes looking straight in front of her, as if daring the open space before her to accept her presence.

"Is he here?"

"He is otherwise occupied, but he is good at delegating; he has Timothy and Titus and Barnabas, among others. There are also some women—Phoebe, Priscilla, Junia, for example—and, of course, Thecla, but that is another story for another time. I transcribe some of his letters for him; I sometimes help him with the composition of them. I soften the hard edges when necessary. He is often busy and sometimes in need of calmness and direction. It was I who made sure you received your invitation."

"You wrote some of the letters?"

"In the first letter to the Corinthians, which I asked him to write, I drafted the sections on marriage and on the quality of the relationship between husbands and wives."

"Are you married?"

"I have my own household, but I am unmarried."

"For the same reason that Paul is?"

"Do you know the Song of Songs?"

"Yes. It's my favourite book of the Old Testament."

"The Old Testament?"

"All Paul's letters will be part of the New Testament."

"Interesting. Anyway, there is more than one way to read the Song of Songs. There is more than one facet to my relationship with Paulos. Tell me, why did you wish to be invited here?"

"I've been given an assignment, so I suppose I'm on my own mission of sorts. It has to do with the first letter to Corinthians, particularly chapter fourteen."

"Chapter fourteen?"

"The section where a distinction is made between prophecy and speaking in tongues."

"All in the context of love—you mustn't forget that."

"How much of that part of the letter was written by Paul and how much by you?"

"As I said, my contribution often has to do with softening the hard edges. He insists that women should be silent in the churches and that they should depend solely on their husbands' knowledge of the message of Jesus, but I managed to at least incorporate, before that, an observation that prophecy, speaking in tongues, faith—any exhortation in those realms depended on love as their foundation."

"And the distinction between prophecy and speaking in tongues?"

"We were in essential agreement about that. What is it that you have been assigned concerning this?"

"My teacher wanted me to dig below the surface to see what truth and beauty I could find there."

"What do you think is the surface?"

"The Christianity of the letter."

"Are you a Christian?"

"I'm interested by Christianity."

"Christianity is young, yet. It is beautiful and it is difficult. Often, these are the same thing. But in the end, it is quite simple; it is true. It is like breathing; one takes in air and one lets out the air. God breathed in the chaos of the unformed world and breathed out Adam. He breathed in the confusion of his creation and he breathed out his son. At the crucifixion, he breathed in his son, and now he breathes out his message in Paulos. He will breathe us in and breathe others out."

Chloe stopped, closed her eyes, leaned her head back, and took a deep breath. She held it in for a few seconds and breathed it out. Violet could not help but do the same. Chloe continued walking, Violet beside her.

"You said you're unmarried but you have your own household—isn't that unusual?"

"These are unusual times."

‡

"I'm beginning to think that I lost more than my virginity."

"Cigarette?" asked Charlotte.

"Yes, thanks."

They had just returned from a long walk along the river, the trees longing for autumn.

"Tell me, what else did you lose?"

"That sense of eternal anticipation that keeps you moving forward."

"This is your perception of the Platonic relationship that you think I have with Jerry?"

"Am I wrong?"

"You're forgetting his daughter, Tina. You said yourself, in your letter to Levi, that my relationship with Tina is really a relationship with my own younger self. If there were no Tina, Jerry could divorce his wife and we could be together, or, to put it in your terms, I could finally reclaim, redeem—whatever verb you care to choose—the young girl abandoned by her mother who never wanted her in the first place—the young girl who was disciplined into a minor madness. Have I managed to summarize the situation adequately?"

"Tina never grows up in this book, does she?"

"We are who we are for all time."

Charlotte and Deborah concentrated on their cigarettes for a long silent minute.

"This is more complicated than you thought," suggested Charlotte. "You first came here to 1930s Boston because you wanted to stop time, as only living in a book can do. But now you want to go back in time—you want to unlose your virginity so that you can continue to anticipate losing it. Perhaps you've chosen the wrong verb. You keep talking of losing, when perhaps you should talk of gaining. You are like Eve biting into the apple—she gains the awareness of her humanity with all its joy and, yes, all its pain. Letting Levi physically into your body as well as spiritually into your heart and intellectually into your head has changed your perception of the world and of yourself in it. Have you not gained something?"

"But what about you? It doesn't seem to me that you feel you need to 'gain' something by losing your virginity—you said so yourself."

"You've been invited into *Now, Voyager*, not into me. Did you want to lose your self rather than your virginity? Where would be the gain in that?"

Deborah crushed her cigarette into the ashtray on the side table and dropped her hands into her lap as if she could no longer figure out what to do with them.

"Levi is with Esther Greenwood," said Deborah, "and he's never going to make love to her. That way he can have her possibility forever."

"Esther and I are cut from the same cloth."

"A richly patterned and textured one."

"A difficultly woven one."

"How else can beauty be rendered?"

"So, Levi is with Esther Greenwood, his eternal possibility. Where is the young Deborah in all this?"

✠

"There are some women I'd like you to meet."

Chloe extended her hand to Violet and led her out of the town square. The sky explained to her what the true meaning of azure was, and the moist breeze off the water was better than any facial she'd ever had. They walked east, out of the city, and they kept walking for a long time. But the conversation made the ten-mile walk seem like a leisurely stroll around the block.

"Once a season, we meet at the pool in the Sanctuary of Isthmia. Phoebe is the deaconess at the church in Cenchrea, the harbour at the eastern edge of Corinth; we will gather her on our way. Priscilla travels by boat from Ephesus, with her husband, Aquila. Junia and Andronicus are emissaries who are continually travelling, but always pass through Corinth for our seasonal meetings. Aquila and Andronicus find something to do while we women gather at the pool."

At Cenchrea, Chloe and Violet stopped in at the house of Phoebe and collected her for the rest of the long walk to the pool.

"Welcome to our church," Phoebe said to Violet.

"Your house is the church?" asked Violet.

"We meet where we can. We sanctify wherever we meet with our presence."

Phoebe was a small woman, like Chloe, but where Chloe had dark hair and eyes, Phoebe had honey-coloured hair and hazel eyes, and where Chloe exuded confidence, Phoebe radiated stillness and comfort.

"Last time, you mentioned Thecla," said Violet, as the three of them continued their journey, "and said that was a story for another time. I'd like to hear that story."

"Ah, Thecla," smiled Phoebe, nodding her head.

"Paulos met Thecla at Iconium," said Chloe, "when he preached at the house of Onesiphorus. You must understand that Paulos has a certain power over women that is not to be explained by his physical beauty, for in the rudimentary descriptive terms of beauty as applied only to the corporeal, he is not a beautiful man; rather, his power comes from the truth he speaks.

It is a seductive truth. At the time when Paulos stayed at the house of Onesiphorous, young Thecla was intended to be married to Thamyris, but she was so stricken by the words of Paulos, that she did not leave the window of her room for three days, listening to this man whom she could not see. Accordingly, Thamyris had it arranged that Paulos should be brought before Castillius, the governor, to have him thrown into prison for the disturbance he was creating, especially among the women. Thecla secretly made her way to the prison and traded her earrings to the turnkey and then a silver looking-glass to the jailer in order that she might sit with Paulos and listen to his teaching. Both Paulos and Thecla were brought again before the governor, who ordered that Paulos be whipped out of the city and Thecla be burned alive.

"Thecla was tied to the stake and the pile was set on fire, but just then the clouds opened and poured rain and hail that extinguished the fire and saved her life. Thecla then followed Paulos to Antioch, though he was reluctant to have her travel with him, not least on account of her great beauty and the consequent danger for her person that that entailed. This danger, of course, came to be, as the magistrate of that city fell in love with her. She denied him in such a way that he was humiliated before his own people, so he ordered that she be thrown naked into a den of lions. The lions, however, would not attack her. She then threw herself into a pool of water to baptize herself in the name of Jesus Christ. Neither did the ravenous beasts that lived in the water attack her, but they died instead. Finally, the governor released her as a servant of God.

"Thence, she searched out Paulos in Myra on the south coast of Lycia. She travelled in the garb of a man to hide her beauty and save her from further persecution because of it. She found Paulos and he decided she should go to teach the word of God in Iconium, from whence she had come. From there, however, she travelled south to Seleucia on the coast. She lives alone on a nearby mountain to this day."

"Lost in praise of God," added Phoebe with a slight note of sarcasm in her voice.

"And of Paulos," said Chloe, but with a sigh of regret and even sadness.

The pool at the Sanctuary of Isthmia was a welcome end to their long walk. Priscilla and Junia were there ahead of them, already standing peacefully in the waist-deep water. The pebble mosaic of the bottom of the pool glimmered through the clear element. Chloe, Phoebe, and Violet stripped themselves of all but the necessary linens to preserve their modesty and waded into the water to form a loose circle with Priscilla and Junia in the middle of the pool.

Violet listened as the four women discussed matters of missions and churches, of collections of clothes and money to support the apostles in their travels from Thessaly and Achaia to Lycia, Pisidia, Pamphylia, Cilicia, and Syria. They also discussed the content of various letters to be sent to all these places, and it was clear to Violet that these women had a greater hand in the epistolary spread of Christianity than was known back in her future time. But Violet wanted to pursue her particular assignment. She wanted to talk about the nature and power, the truth and beauty, of language as communication.

"Paulos," said Phoebe, "has studied the art of rhetoric, especially that of Aristotle. But where Aristotle is a great analytic thinker and has, sometimes, even an insightful psychic comprehension, his understanding of the soul does not approach our understanding of the spirit as it relates to God, the father, and his son, Jesus Christ. Still, Aristotle understands the power of language, and without that, our missions to both the Gentiles and the Jews would be inadequate to open people's minds and hearts."

"In the end," said Chloe, returning to Violet's concern with prophecy and speaking in tongues, "prophecy, speaking with the mind, is preferable to speaking in tongues, which is speaking with the spirit and, therefore, most often too personal, too oriented to God rather than to humans."

"There is much to be learned from many uses of language—Sophocles's plays, for example. From Antigone I learn that fanaticism must be tempered with patience; it must be fired in the crucible of greater intention. Love must light that flame," said Priscilla.

"I," said Junia, bobbing in the warm water, "have learned much from Penelope, Dido, Ariadne, Briseis, Medea, among others, in Ovid's Heroides, those wonderful epistolary poems for which there is no literary precedent. These women write of abandonment and longing, of suffering and hope—in the end, of grief, which I sometimes prefer over the guarantee of the resurrected life that Jesus offers us. There is truth and beauty in both."

Violet wondered how young she really was. It was hard to tell the ages of any of these four women.

"This teacher of yours," said Chloe, "what does he teach?"

"He teaches me to be more than myself."

"To what end?"

"I don't know that. I can't know that. I don't think he can know that either."

"No guarantees, then," said Junia. "An honest man."

"Perhaps," suggested Priscilla, "his assignment for you concerns the nature of teaching. Let me ask you, then, how you understand prophecy and speaking in tongues."

"I understand the language of the mind as opposed to the language of the spirit, but I'm not sure there should be a distinction. If someone cannot understand a person who speaks in tongues, perhaps the fault lies with the listener and not the speaker."

"Do you think we should send her to Thecla?" Phoebe asked of the other women.

‡

Late September. *Sukkot*, the autumn harvest festival—*hag ha-asif*, in which the custom is to dwell in temporary booths. One of the three major pilgrimage festivals. What was this pilgrimage she was on, wondered Deborah. What kind of voyager was she, and was this book meant only to be her temporary dwelling? The reading for this part of the liturgical cycle was

Ecclesiastes—*Koheleth*, the arguer, the haranguer. A Wisdom book. Wisdom through experience. She was gathering experience, but was she gathering wisdom?

The opening lines of Ecclesiastes—all about *hevel*: breath, human breath, that transitory thing about which Job says to God after he has been afflicted, "I am sick of it. I shall not live forever; let me be, for my days are but a breath." Or *hevel*: vanity, futility—"Utter futility!—said Koheleth—Utter futility! All is futile!" Life, breath—the futility of these transitory things. And yet, Deborah is drawn to this haranguer, this preacher, this wisdom bringer, because he experiences his own life and the lives of those around him and he tells it like it is—the natural cycles of life, the power and emptiness of wealth, friendship as an antidote to the uncertainties of life, the nature of folly, the possibilities and limitations of wisdom, the terror of old age, the inevitability of death. If there is an afterlife, we can't know what it is: "There is nothing worthwhile for a man but to eat and drink and afford himself enjoyment with his means."

"Is that the Jewish version of 'Eat, drink, and be merry, for tomorrow we may die'?" asked Charlotte.

"In so many words, yes," said Deborah.

"Is that from the Bible?"

"Ecclesiastes."

"I haven't had much use of it. Nevertheless, you think I have taken this as my motto?"

"A version of it, yes."

"I would like to think of the aphorism—you don't mind that I refer to a biblical passage as an aphorism?—as somehow more comforting, even more promising, than that. I would like to think that I have gained—you see how important that word is—some wisdom through my experience."

"You're playing with me. You *have* read Ecclesiastes."

"I read many things. I've always loved to read, beginning with *Sara Crewe* all the way up to . . . well, I like to read when I have the time. But I do not read to escape; I read to arrive somewhere," said Charlotte, flashing Deborah a mischievous smile.

"Do you live that way, too?"

"Oh, no. Life is already a destination, but there is much to explore while we're here. Would you like to take a drive?"

"Vermont?"

"Let's be adventurous—drive somewhere neither of us has been."

‡

Junia volunteered to accompany Violet on her journey to Seleucia to find Thecla.

"I'm anxious to be out on the sea again. Too much time with my feet on solid ground sometimes seems to anchor my spirit, which is why I enjoy the pool in the Sanctuary of Isthmia as much as I do. I would also like to find out for once and all if Thecla truly exists. I often feel that Chloe and Priscilla try to take advantage of my adventures of the spirit by telling me stories that are beautiful but not, perhaps, true."

Violet and Junia travelled for several days by boat from Corinth to Seleucia, making stops at Patmos, Rhodes, Myra, and Salamis on the way. Violet discovered that she had the opposite perception of land and water that Junia had. She was glad to get her feet under her on solid ground once again. Once arrived at Seleucia, they made their way to Mount Calamon north of the city in search of Thecla, whose existence many in Seleucia vouched for.

"She lives alone in a cave in the mountain," said one Seleucian. "She does nothing but pray. We sometimes bring her food," said another. "She may or may not acknowledge your presence," said yet another. "She is a holy virgin. She will know if you have come with purity of intention."

"Some women treat their virginity as a holy affliction," said Junia to Violet as they walked out of the city. "Are you thus afflicted?"

"No."

The day was hot and dusty, and by the time they had climbed to within sight of Thecla's cave, they were tired and thirsty.

"Should we just walk up to the entrance to the cave?" asked Violet.

"Why else are we here?"

In spite of her seeming swagger, Junia waited for Violet to move towards the cave, then followed along behind her. Just as Violet was about to lean into the darkness of the opening, a woman appeared before them. She eyed the two visitors with an intensity that comes only of days, weeks, months spent in silence and contemplation.

"You," she said, nodding towards Violet. "You may come in first."

She turned and disappeared into the darkness of the cave. The darkness, however, was deceptive. Once Violet was inside the cave, it was as easy to see the contours and texture of her surroundings as if she were in the broad daylight. She turned to look back at the entrance to the cave to see how this could be. It was at that moment that Thecla spoke to her.

"You are not from this time."

"No."

"Nor am I, in common understanding. Why have you come?"

"I am curious."

"Curiosity may be composed of seeking or of temptation. You have the air of one who has been tempted."

"Perhaps."

"By a man?"

"Yes."

"I have been with men, but I have preserved myself in their company. I preserve myself for the one in whose name Paulos preaches. Here," she said, waving her arm towards the space around her, "I am better able to face temptation, for there is no one else to deflect it from me. There is no one else who can preserve me from it. One can hear the teachings, one can espouse them, but one must face temptation alone, as did Christ in the desert. This is my desert. Are you in search of your desert?"

"I am in search of knowledge."

"We must have faith in that which we cannot know. Like Paulos, we must put ourselves in the way of revelation. For each of us, it will come in a different way. For each of us, it will have a different consequence."

"Can you tell me about the difference between prophecy and speaking in tongues?"

"The letter to the Corinthians. Prophecy—the language of the mind, the message that can be communicated to the masses. Speaking in tongues—the language of the spirit, individual to each spirit, yet common to God. Prophecy cannot be unless there is first speaking in tongues. What God says to each of us as individuals is more important than what the prophets say in His name."

Thecla bowed her head and seemed to forget the presence of Violet in her cave. Violet was not sure whether to stay and wait, or take her leave. She waited, then rose to her feet and turned to leave. As she reached the mouth of the cave, Thecla spoke one last time.

"There is another you should seek."

Violet stepped out of the cave light into the sunlight.

"Well?" said Junia.

"Do you know where Magdala is?"

‡

Early one morning in late September, Deborah put her suitcase, along with Charlotte's and Tina's and Tina herself, in the back seat of Charlotte's pepper-tan Hudson Terraplane, the most comfortable and luxurious car Deborah had ever ridden in. Sitting in the front seat was like sitting on a sofa in someone's living room. Why did they not make cars like this anymore?

"Cape Cod or bust," said Charlotte with as much excitement as the young Tina experiencing the independence of travel for the first time. "This will be even better than the cruise. I can feel as if I'm truly in motion. There were times on that great liner when I felt a sense of stillness I had never experienced before. It was as if I were imprisoned in a motionlessness that would suffocate me. It got better, though, once I allowed myself to be social. Then I was in motion, and the ship could take care of itself."

Tina took it upon herself to be the narrator of their journey, constantly pointing out every major and minor spectacle on either side of the road as they drove along. Deborah was assigned the task of navigating, map spread out on her knees. When they reached Plymouth, the map told her, though she could not verify it accurately with her own eyes, that due east across Cape Cod Bay was the town of Wellfleet, halfway up the forearm of the Cape, considering Sandwich as the shoulder, Orleans as the elbow, North Truro as the wrist, and Provincetown as the curled hand.

They stopped for tea and sandwiches in Barnstable, Tina narrating the appearance and consumption of their simple repast as if the Lord had rained down bread from the heaven for Moses and his weary followers. After Dennis and towards Brewster, Tina's narrative dwindled in volubility as the country became wilder and less easeful to human presence. While Tina was not sure how daring she should allow herself to be as they left behind the comforts of civilization as she had come to know them in her young life, Charlotte's eyes grew brighter; her whole aspect seemed to shimmer with expectation. For her part, Deborah contemplated her double journey—in this car on a Cape Cod road with Charlotte and Tina, and in this book, a voyager in time as well as space.

They motored into and through Orleans to Eastham, where they parked the car and walked across to Nauset Beach and the lighthouse. Sand became the currency of the landscape, and dunes the rise and fall of the speculative wind. The three of them began hand in hand, Tina between Charlotte and Deborah, but Tina needed to rush more quickly into the wilds of this pleasantly alien world, having left behind her apprehensions and acclimatized herself before she had time to consider that that was what she had done. Charlotte and Deborah widened the space between them until all three arrived in sight of the ocean in their own bubbles of consciousness. There it was—the Atlantic coast where the horizon was nothing but sky and water so vast that Deborah felt she was standing on the edge of infinity. She thought of Moses, who, after struggling through deserts of sand and hope, stood in sight of the Promised Land, which he would not get to experience. But then she recalled Ecclesiastes: "Send your bread forth upon the waters; for after many days you will find it," and "Just as you do not know how the lifebreath passes into the limbs within the womb of the pregnant woman, so you cannot foresee the actions of God, who causes all things to happen. Sow your seed in the morning, and don't hold back your hand in the evening, since you don't know which is going to succeed, the one or the other, or if both are equally good." Wise old codger, she thought as she smiled herself into the wind and the crashing surf.

‡

"She said her name?"
"Yes."
"Did she say she was in Magdala?"
"She said, 'Look for Mary where she came from.'"

Junia had heard of Mary of Magdala—who among the fledgling Christians had not? No one knew where she had gone after the Resurrection; no one knew if she was still alive. Junia would have given anything to speak with the women who had witnessed the crucifixion or the Resurrection. Though she was dedicated in her spirit to the teachings of Jesus as they were interpreted by Paul, she was hungry to stand in the presence of one who was a witness to the deeds and not just to the reverberations of them. Mary, the mother of Jesus, had recently died, according to the word of those who were supposed to know. As for Salome, Junia had heard from a reliable source who had heard from a reliable source that she had conversed with Jesus on many occasions and had asked him about death and eternal life. She wanted to know how long death would prevail on Earth, to which Jesus was said to reply that it would prevail as long as women bore children. Salome was said to have chosen to remain a virgin for the rest of her days, though no one knew where she had decided to pass those days. And now, here was this woman from some foreign time and place who had been advised by Thecla that Mary of Magdala not only lived, but could be found.

"Magdala is by the Sea of Galilee, many weeks from here by foot, but only many days by water if we sail to Ptolemais."

"Can you take me there?" asked Violet.

Violet had chosen Corinth because she thought she needed to meet Paul, but very quickly she had become impressed by the women who followed him, supported him, even helped create him in the eyes of others, in the same way that he helped to create Jesus in the eyes of others. Violet believed that whether these women understood it or not, they had their own power beyond the message they were disseminating. She wanted that power, too.

‡

"You're not coming back once you leave this time, are you?"

Charlotte blew out a long stream of smoke as she leaned across the coffee table to light Deborah's cigarette.

"I was hoping to introduce you to Jerry and to Dr. Jaquith, but you have your own Jerry to get back to. Do you have a Dr. Jaquith?"

"I think I've always been my own Dr. Jaquith—that's the rabbi part of myself."

"And the other part?"

"I don't think that I've ever consciously tried to forfeit my womanhood in order to understand God or to explain to others how they might understand him, but neither did I nurture it."

"Sometimes, perhaps most times, we need to be invited to feed that part of ourselves. We need to be honoured for being women—individual women, not representations of women."

"I think that's why I came here—to hear another woman confirm that for me."

"My experience is not your experience, though."

"Virginity, you mean?"

"Virginity is an experience in the same way that giving up your virginity is an experience. The nature of possibility changes, but there is always possibility. Your possibility is now a different one from mine. Perhaps I will come to visit you to see how your possibility develops."

"I would love to put you and Levi in a room together and just observe like a fly on the wall."

"It does no good to just be an observer. But you already know that."

"Yes, I do know that. But sometimes . . ."

"Let's go for one last walk by the river."

They put on their coats and scarves, an autumn chill in the air. They strolled the couple of blocks down to the river, smoking lazily along the shore towards the Harvard Bridge. The evening was drawing down and the lights of the city began to sprout in the settling darkness. They walked out on the bridge, stopping halfway along to lean on the railing and look down at the water passing beneath them on its way to the ocean. Deborah thought about how everything leads to the ocean, in one way or another. The emptying of wandering, twisting currents of nature and imagination into the vastness of mystery. Charlotte remembered her cruise out of her confined self into her open self. They smoked their cigarettes down, then flicked them into the river where they disappeared. They turned and hugged each other.

‡

Junia proposed they wait for a ship to take them from Seleucia to Tyre or Ptolemais, but they would have to postpone the voyage for a few weeks because she was needed back in Corinth. The more Violet thought about it, however, the clearer she became about three decisions: she wanted to begin her journey immediately, she wanted to walk from Seleucia to Magdala, and she wanted to go alone.

"It will take you thirty days at the very least," cautioned Junia. "That is a long way to travel alone, especially as a woman."

Violet was not to be discouraged or deflected. When she bade goodbye to Junia, she said she hoped to see her again. Junia at least prepared her for the journey by outfitting her with the proper clothes and sandals and provisions.

Violet set out along the coast northwest to Tarsus, a journey of four days. There she arranged for enough food and water to take her to Antioch, about eight days distance. She developed a rhythm that was nothing like she had ever experienced. She did not think about the soreness of her feet or the punishing heat at midday or the absence of a companion; she was of her body but not in it. If there were such a thing as meditative bliss, she was inside it for most of each day. Instead of anticipating those parts of the day when she could stop moving, when she could rest and eat and drink, she looked forward to releasing herself to the meditative motion of walking. Everything—how she had come to be where she was, why she had chosen to be here, friends, family, Professor Pepperfield, day-to-day obligations of living—all of it fell away, leaving in its place the overwhelming present.

At Antioch she decided to rest for a couple of days and replenish both her body and her determination. While there she managed to find some Hellenists who had been Christianized and taken up residence in the city. They advised her that she might have an easier journey to the Sea of Galilee if she followed the river system south of Antioch, beginning on the Orontes. At least, she would not have to worry about water to drink, which, if she had to choose, was more important than food to eat on a regular basis.

Twenty-four days later, she arrived at Lake Huleh. From there it was a half day's journey south along the River Jordan to the Sea of Galilee, then another half day's journey to Magdala on the western shore of the Sea. On one side the layered hills rising to the white-blue sky; on the other the slope towards green trees and the dusty blue of the Sea of Galilee. She walked through low-walled streets, past the synagogue, past the ritual baths, trying all the while to convince herself of where she was, of whom she was about to meet. She decided to find a place for the night and begin her search for Mary in the morning.

All she had to go on was the name Mary Magdalene—Mary from the city of Magdala. That, of course, would apply to any woman named Mary who lived in the city.

"I am looking for Mary who was an apostle of Jesus and who was at his crucifixion."

She had to ask five different people before she received a very reluctant direction to her dwelling. It was not that no one knew who she was; rather, everyone knew and they all wanted to protect her identity. As Violet would find out, Mary did not want to advertise herself or her connection with Jesus. She looked nothing like the hundreds of representations Violet had seen of her in paintings. Violet wished she had some of those pictures to show Mary; she was the kind of woman who would have smiled with amusement at them.

"Why do you seek me?" she asked Violet.

There was a tone of guarded curiosity in her voice; clearly, she had had to ask this question many times before. When Violet explained that she had been directed here by Thecla, Mary relaxed, though she maintained a composure that bespoke a kind of self-confidence and patience that came with hard-won wisdom.

"You are neither from this place nor this time," observed Mary.

"No."

"What is it you are searching for?"

"My tongue; my self."

"Jesus often spoke of that search. He said that all searches began and ended there, though when you returned, you would return to a self you did not know you were."

The compound word *self-knowledge* was not found in the Oxford English Dictionary until 1613; *self-seeker* in 1632; *self-examination* in 1647; *self-knowing* in 1677.

"Though many of us believed in what he said, none of us could truly understand him because though we had the words, we did not yet have the experience. There was hardly time for us to gain it before he was crucified."

"Do you have the experience now?" asked Violet.

"You need to transform the words into your own experiences and your own wisdom. Belief without the understanding of your own lived life cannot sustain the message, no matter whose message it is. People can preach all they want, but it is the example of their lives, not their words, that will save us. Let us go to the baths," said Mary.

They walked in slow silence, comfortable silence. Sitting in the hot baths, their silence continued, though it became more clearly defined, more clearly textured.

"Did you know him for a long time?" asked Violet. "Did you know him well?"

"We understood each other as corporeal and as spiritual beings..."

Part Six

*There are doors
that want to be free
from their hinges to
fly with perfect clouds*
—Richard Brautigan

*Dear Professor Pepperfield,
    I've completed my assignment.
Violet*

‡

*More than ever dearest Levi,
    I'm coming back. You?
Prodigal Deborah*

‡

"Interesting letters?"

Elbows on the table, shoulders hunched, hands curved around her mug of hot apple cider like a child holding a treasure she has just found and is afraid of losing, Esther looked up at me. Her eyes glistened, the way eyes do when they are on the edge of tears, be they of happiness or sorrow.

"Very short letters."

"Sometimes the fewer words, the better."

She took a sip of her hot apple cider, then placed the mug on the table in front of her. It made the sound of something closing and opening at the same time.

"You're eternally wounded," she said.

She paused, letting the content of the words catch up to their brevity.

"You're eternally dying," she added.

Another pause, this time to allow me to catch up to the content.

"As long as you choose to stay here, you can never be healed and you can never die. Do you understand that?"

"What about you? What if you choose to stay here?"

"Let's deal with you first. Do you still not recognize this place?" she asked, waving her arm at the space all around us.

I wanted to say yes, but I couldn't say anything.

"Do you not understand a living metaphor when you see it? Your desire is to never grow old. Your wound is that you have grown old. This book, it's the centre of the labyrinth, a moving, shifting labyrinth, and you have no ball of red thread and no packet of matches. I use matches now, but I did use a thread at the end of *The Bell Jar*. But you don't need thread or matches. Remember the image of the kaleidoscope you chose for your dissertation? Rotate the tube, Levi. That's how you get different worlds."

Esther pushed her empty mug to the centre of the table with one hand and put her other hand on top of mine.

"Rotate it until you find the end of *The Bell Jar*. Wait for me at the front door of the asylum and I'll come out and meet you."

‡

"Sometimes a soldier stands up from where he has fallen down and the world doesn't look the same. Oh, it has the same trees, the same sky, but when he takes a deep breath he can feel the difference. Then he passes his hand over his body and it comes back up to his face moistened with blood, and for a moment he can't believe it's his own blood. Put your hand up to your face, old boy. Your soul is bleeding."

He was sitting by my bed, his white beard drifting down over his shirt into the V of his vest, his cane hooked over the back of the chair. I lifted my head from the pillow, disoriented.

"'And if the body were not the soul, what is the soul?'" said the man from the other side of my bed, his yellow blonde moustache drooping over the corners of his mouth, his broad-brimmed slouch hat slouching on his head as if it had settled there a long, long time ago. "Not enough people get that," he said, reaching his hand across my body towards old whitebeard.

> "'The sweet juices of your mouth
> are like castles bathed in honey,
> I've never had it done so gently before.
> You have put a circle of castles
> around my penis and you swirl them
> like sunlight on the wings of birds'

"—not enough men get that, either, I suppose."

He, likewise, extended his hand across my body. They shook hands somewhere over my chest.

"I wrote that for Marcia Pacaud."

"I know," I tried to say, but my tongue felt like a foreign object in my mouth. "She's on the cover of *The Pill Versus The Springhill Mine Disaster*," I mumbled. My voice was exhausted, my eyes were heavy, my arm was around Esther, who seemed lost in sleep beside me.

"Forever young," said the man in the slouch hat looking down at Esther. "That's the way to be. That's why I put a bullet in my head."

He looked up at the moon shining down on the three of us and sighed. It pooled in his round glasses.

"Marcia Pacaud, she was beautiful," I groaned.

"She's much older now," said old whitebeard. "You recalibrate beauty to accord with truth as you get older."

"I'm going fishing," said the droopy-moustachioed poet. "There's nothing else I can do here. You can have this if you need it," he said, looking at me.

He placed a nickel-plated Smith & Wesson Model 28 revolver on the bedside table before he left the room.

"It's my anniversary today," he said to some abstract space above and behind me.

"He didn't even recognize me," said the woman as she walked into the room carrying a steaming cup of coffee in each hand. She was somewhere between willowy and sturdy, with long hair, once blonde, parted in the middle and hanging past her shoulders like Spanish moss on a Southern Live Oak. All the features of her face were long and thin or wide and thin—her nose, her mouth, her eyes.

"Marcia Pacaud?" I asked with my heavy-lidded eyes.

"I hope you like it black," she said to the old poet as she handed him one of the cups.

"I could use some coffee," I pleaded with makeshift sounds. "Esther could use some coffee."

"He's not good at calibrating possibility with manifestation," said the old poet about the man who had just left the room. "He left that," he said jutting his chin towards the revolver on the night table on the other side of my bed.

"He wrote me some beautiful poems," she said, seating herself next to the night table on the opposite side of my bed from the old poet. "He used words like shields to protect himself from a world he thought he could manipulate into submission. Another of your wounded and dying soldiers?" she asked, looking down at me.

"Soldiers come in all manner of guises," he said.

"And her?"

"Her, too. Now, the soldiers I'm most familiar with are those poor young men—and the occasional surprising young woman—yes, some of them, the very unusually brave ones, eventually had to surrender their disguises when they ended up in the field hospitals—I'm most familiar with those poor young soldiers who fought for and against the Union, though too many of them had no idea what the true ideals of each side were. They were all, in one way or another, shrapnelled with the consequences of misdirected desire. They mistook youth for immortality. I have held their hands as they died in the irony of that mistake."

He reached out his hand to place it on mine, but Esther, suddenly aroused, pushed it away.

"They've got life in them yet," Marcia Pacaud said. "She's the one he wrote the letter to?"

"Yes."

"Am I next?"

"Quite possibly. The problem is, he doesn't yet know how to keep his worlds separate. Best to wait for a while."

"Richard wasn't any good at that, either. Do you think Levi, here, would want me like this?" she asked, using the hand that didn't have the coffee cup in it to wave across her body. "I'm older than even he is. Fewer possibilities than when I was on the cover."

"Appearance must not foil, nor shifted sphere confuse thy brain."

"Sounds like a line from a poem. Yours?"

"We can only write our own poetry."

"Or be a muse to those who do."

"Good coffee," said old whitebeard.

"Refill?"

"It's probably time we went on our way."

He leaned slowly to put his empty cup down on the floor beside his chair. Unfolding himself back to sitting position, he paused before standing up to unhook his cane from the back of the chair. She put her cup on the night table, moving the gun to make room for it. She walked around to the other side of the bed and offered her arm to old whitebeard. He thanked her with a smile. They began to make their way towards the door.

"Would you like to see where the photo was taken?" she asked him. "There might be a poem in it for you."

"Well, you know, it just so happens . . ." and their voices faded away down the stairs.

Part Seven

*I have heard what the talkers were talking,
the talk of the beginning and the end,
But I do not talk of the beginning or the end.*
    —*Walt Whitman*

THE LANDSCAPE WAS much the same, but I was aware of subtle differences. I seemed to be under a different part of the sky's canopy; the clouds stretched themselves into slightly different shapes; the air had a top note of ocean in it; the sun coloured the trees with a touch more light here, a touch less light there. I stood outside the front door of the asylum, my collar turned up against the sun-sparkled chill of winter, the January sun emphasizing rather than tempering the cold air. The doors opened with slow reluctance, like the skin on the fleshy part of your thumb giving up a sliver after several days of harbouring it like some fugitive. She stood on the steps and let the doors close with relief behind her. She paused there, looking first at me, then up at the sky, then back down at me. Her face grew a smile as she walked down the steps, her feet savouring each minor descent towards level ground.

"I wasn't sure you'd come," she said.

"Neither was I."

"Second thoughts?"

"Second worlds. Or third, or fourth."

"You brought your kaleidoscope with you, then?"

"I'm not sure it's my kaleidoscope. So, we're in *The Bell Jar*?"

"The bell jar has been lifted. The air is rushing in. Take a deep breath."

She closed her eyes, leaned her head back under the weight of the breath inspired into her lungs.

"I've been deemed patched, retreaded, and approved for the road."

"Sounds like an old tire."

"I know. I need a better image for having been born twice. You're the professor—any suggestions?"

"Beyond the labyrinth and the kaleidoscope?"

"You can never have enough metaphors."

"Are you sure about that? What if metaphors are like the figs you talked about—you choose one, and all the others are denied you?"

"I've decided to no longer be denied. So, offer me a metaphor for my new life."

"Are you still considering writing your thesis on *Finnegan's Wake*?"

"Do you think I could survive it?"

"I think you can't resist it."

"Have you taught it?"

"Whenever I try to read it, I feel as if I'm shoving my head into a meat grinder."

"We could teach it to each other."

"You talk of being born twice. Do you mean to distinguish that from being reborn?"

"You mean, do I carry any part of who I used to be into who I want to be?"

"Perhaps I mean the difference between resurrection and reconfiguration."

"How about transfiguration?"

"Okay, transfiguration."

"You're sidestepping my request for a new metaphor."

"Well, I mentioned *Finnegan's Wake* because it's a kind of circle—the book gets born again in its ending. The first sentence of the book can be read as the completion of the last incomplete sentence of the book— 'A way a lone a last a loved a long the riverrun, past Eve and Adam's, from swerve of shore to bend of bay, brings us by a commodious vicus of recirculation back to

Howth Castle and Environs.' I think it's interesting that you want to take up the challenge of *Finnegan's Wake* again, as if you're circling back to it, the way it circles back on itself."

"But I won't be the same person I was when I first came to the book. The book is the same, but I'm not. So, my metaphor, please."

"Lingual buckshot."

"Lingual buckshot?"

"That's what we are, as long as we're in a book. Each of us is a tiny pellet exploding out of the shell, out of the tongue, or the pen, of the writer."

"And I, as the writer of my thesis, would be scattering my buckshot words across the page."

"Forget my metaphor. I don't think you should write a thesis on *Finnegan's Wake*."

"Why not?"

"You can't put all the pellets back in the shell once it's been fired."

"So, you think I should choose some other literary work. Which one would you suggest?"

"Forget the thesis. Write poetry."

"But what about graduating?"

"You just graduated by walking out those doors."

"But I'm good at being a student. I can get A's in any subject, even mathematics and physics."

"If you want to be a real student, get as far away from an academic institution as you can. They're just differently configured asylums."

"You sound rather jaded. Don't project that on me."

"You want me to offer you a metaphor. I'm offering you the fruits of my experience instead. Don't you think that's more valuable?"

"It's not my experience. I have to have my own experience. You can't save me from that."

"I'm not trying to save you."

"Of course you are. You're trying to save me because you couldn't save yourself. You want to live your life through me in this world, but it's my world. You can observe it, you can walk around in it, but you can't control it."

The sound of snow crunching under our boots; the sound of words crunching in our mouths.

"Instead of me dropping out of college, why don't you reintroduce yourself to it from my side of the desk?"

"I've already been on your side of the desk."

"Not at sixty-something, you haven't. Not in 1955, you haven't. Not with me, you haven't. Not in this book, you haven't. What's the point of being here if you're not going to see the world from a different perspective? Maybe truth isn't what you think it is. Or beauty, either."

She was right, of course, but I was instinctively reluctant. I knew what the system did to people, from both sides of the desk. But then, this was Harvard she was talking about. If nothing else, I could soak up the architecture and the aura of the place.

"Let yourself be seduced," Esther said, knocking her shoulder against mine.

‡

All university classrooms, especially in those universities established in the nineteenth century, exude the innocence and gush of youthful expectation, the unconsciously spiritual aspiration of that youth, the quiet intensity of the curious mind that hangs in the air, that seeps up out of the tiered wooden desks, that rises from the stage where the professor stands like Cnut the Great before the tide of the generation that will one day overwhelm him in spite of himself. It was all this I felt as I walked into the room where Esther's class on Techniques of Poetry met.

I was reminded of my first day of university—Riverdene University, established in 1878, hallowed with traditions of learning that were as mysterious to me as a naked woman. It was my first time living away from home, and I was as excited as I was fearful. I held the world in awe during those first days; I was willing to sacrifice myself on the altar of all that was mysterious and, therefore, desirable. I carried home my textbooks from the bookstore as if their very weight and physicality were already instilling me with the secret knowledge that would transform me into a character in a book I would want to read. Too quickly did that electricity overload my circuits, and, as effortlessly intelligent as I was in the elementary and secondary arenas of learning, I was left with only one live wire that maintained the connection between the romanticism of expectation and the reality of academia: poetry and story. All my concepts, conscious and unconscious, of truth and beauty danced along those wires, shorting now one, now another, shooting out random sparks that landed in the eyes of young women I encountered in my classes, or on walks between college buildings, or on the downtown sidewalks, igniting there another kind of dance altogether, one that I could admire only from a distance. I could feel the rhythms of that long-stilled dance begin to vibrate in me again as I sat down next to Esther amidst the gentle thud of books on desks, the rustle of winter-coated bodies on chairs, the thick clatter of voices in every direction.

"You feel it, don't you?" said Esther, leaning her head close to mine, as she pulled her gloves off and set them beside her book on the desk.

What I felt was Esther as pure possibility.

The professor entered from stage right, the door through which he walked creaking with three centuries of tradition, closing behind him with the muffle of thousands of students' expectations. He reached centre stage, stood in front of his pulpit, placing his notes carefully, exaggeratedly before him, stared out and up at the rows of eyes and ears hushed in anticipation. He let the silence settle upon the room like the cloud that settled on Mount Sinai as Moses awaited the word of God.

"'Where every word is at home,'" he began, as if he had already begun his sentence in the silence, "'Taking its place to support the others, the word neither diffident nor ostentatious,'" (which he certainly was at this moment, but effectively so) "'An easy commerce of the old and the new.'"

He paused again, the silence now almost palpable.

"T.S. Eliot, from the final section of the final Quartet. 'An easy commerce of the old and the new.' There is old knowledge and there is new knowledge. Both these kinds of knowledge will be our goal in this course, as it has always and necessarily been for any true poet. The true poet knows well the tradition from which he comes, and he knows well that the blood of that tradition must mix with the blood of his own time. But the poet is not his poem; the poem is not the poet. The poet is but a catalyst; the poet, as Eliot affirms, must continually surrender himself 'as he is at the moment to something which is more valuable. The progress of the artist,' he avows, 'is a continual self-sacrifice, a continual extinction of personality.'"

Much as I admired Eliot's poetry, especially the Four Quartets, concerning which I had written my doctoral dissertation, I could sense Whitman turning very uncomfortably in his grave. The tweed-jacketed professor reached into his pocket, took out a straight-stemmed pipe, the bowl of which had already been filled with tobacco, set it determinedly in the corner of his mouth while extracting a box of wooden matches from the opposite pocket. A flare of light—the sound of the match scraping the side of the box and hissing into flame reached even the last rows of the theatre—calmed itself so that he could hold it carefully over the bowl of tobacco. He puffed out a few clouds of smoke and continued his lecture, dripping in personality, an irony which he refused to acknowledge.

"The mind of the poet is the catalyst, operating on the life experience of the poet. But the man who suffers is distinctly separate from the mind of the poet who creates. You would do well to heed this insightful observation of one of our greatest poets."

At this point, if I were standing on that stage—I would have dispensed with the pulpit—I would have pointed out that no matter how great a poet Eliot was, his voice, particularly his literary theoretical voice, was just one voice among many, and any beginning poet should be wary of wearing his words like an anchor. I would have thrown open the discussion to the class. All the students in this class were too spellbound by the authority of the professor. They did not wonder for a minute where that authority came from; all they knew was that they needed to grow into that authority one day if they wanted to be validated human beings, never mind successful poets. I wished that the professor had quoted that part of Eliot's article that said, "it is not desirable to confine knowledge to whatever can be put into a useful shape for examinations." I wish that he would have set that statement alongside Whitman's adjuration to "no longer take things at second or third hand, nor look through the eyes of the dead, nor feed on the spectres in books." Now there would have been an interesting discussion.

"Did you buy all that stuff about the extinction of personality?" I asked Esther as we sat at the counter in The Tasty in Harvard Square.

It reminded me a little of my own favourite diner at the gates of Riverdene. Esther had shrugged off her coat and draped it over the stool next to her. She was sliding her hands back and forth on the side of her coffee cup.

"Do I dare disagree with T.S. Eliot, you mean?"

"Yeah."

"I do now. I wouldn't have a year ago."

"Why didn't you speak up in class?"

"I'll let my poetry speak for itself."

"As opposed to speaking for you?"

"Me, the poem—it's all the same thing."

"As in, we are the words in the book?"

"If you want."

"What do you want?"

"To be well written. To be the still unravished bride of quietness. What do you want?"

"Some cinnamon toast."

‡

"'What mad pursuit? What struggle to escape?
What pipes and timbrels? What wild ecstasy?'"

The weight of a thousand dead poets pressed down on my chest. I was sweating, trying to lift my head from the pillow, trying to direct my eyes to the voice navigating its way through that swamp of spirits to reach my hungry ears.

"Esther?"

"Dear, sweet Levi."

"Where are you? I can hear you, but . . ."

"'Heard melodies are sweet, but those unheard. Are sweeter.' You've always known this. This is what has always kept your life moving forward."

Her voice grew fainter. I could sense her outline at the foot of my bed, but only in my peripheral vision. Whenever I tried to focus my eyes on her, she would be apparent only as the echo of smoke that cannot command a constant shape.

"It's time for me to go," her voice said.

"Not yet. Please. Can I go back with you?"

"They're waiting for you, Levi."

"Who?"

"There is no beginning; there is no end. I'll find you . . ."

Part Eight

*Yes! it's true all my visions
have come home to roost at last.
They are all true now and stand
around me like a bouquet of
lost ships and doomed generals.*
 —*Richard Brautigan*

My body felt like a pile of scrap lumber. First, I tried to unlock my knee joints, inch by inch stretching out my legs, not sure if the whining hinge sound was coming from them or from the porch swing on which I was sitting. I opened and closed my fingers, those of my right hand releasing the coffee cup they'd been clutching. The dark stain on my pant leg suggested the contents of the cup had been tipped there some time ago—it was cold and clammy. Slowly, I saved the joints of my body from incipient rigor mortis. I was, indeed, sprawled on the porch swing, the sun of a cool autumn day somewhere in the middle of its arc. How long I'd been asleep, I had no idea. From the stiffened condition of my body, it could have been eighteen or twenty-four hours or more. After three tries, I achieved standing position, which I held for a good long minute before attempting ambulation. The next hour was comprised of a stumbling entry into my house, a hot shower, a change into fresh warm clothes, a plate of sausages and eggs and toast, and a freshly perked pot of coffee.

For all of this time since I'd resurrected myself, I could feel the echo of that world with Esther in it in the very core of my being. I had been catapulted out of it before I was ready and I wondered now, between sips of oh so beautifully perked coffee, how I could get back there, whether I should go back there, whether it was a real possible world at all. The last thing I remembered about that world was a desire for cinnamon toast. Sated as I was by the breakfast, or lunch, or whatever it was that I had just eaten, I was not sated in that part of me that only cinnamon toast could sate. I put on my jacket and aimed myself towards the diner at the gates of Riverdene.

I examined every woman I passed to see if she might be Esther, knowing in the rational part of my brain that it was impossible for her to be here in the flesh, but there is that part of the brain that cannot be controlled by the rigid strictures and scriptures of the so-called rational mind. I was still not ready to consider the apparently simple realities of Deborah and Violet. Cinnamon toast might serve as a bridge back to them.

"Taking the sidewalk today, Mister Pepperfield."

This observation came from the person standing beside me as I was about to cross the fabled five-street intersection in the center of town. It was the policeman who had interviewed me on the occasion of my saunter down the middle of Charter Street in the middle of the night.

"The middle of the road is for the middle of the night, when one is lubricated with fine whiskey and dismissive of the social conventions of daylight hours," I replied.

"I tried it, you know. The very next night."

"Under the security of immunity from prosecution?"

"Under the curiosity of a man who is considering possible activities for retirement."

"What will you do during daylight hours?"

"My wife will organize that for me, I'm sure. You married?"

"No. Do you recommend it?"

"Depends on the day you ask me. Most days I'd say yes, with the proviso that you proceed with caution. So, you've never been married?"

"I neither sought it or nor avoided it. It just didn't happen, though I'm pretty sure that was a good thing for all considered. A day off, I presume? Or are you working undercover?"

"Technically, it's a day off, but cops are always at the ready. Downside of the job, I suppose. We always carry ongoing and unsolved cases around in our heads, no matter how hard we try to relax. For instance, there's this all-night restaurant on one of those side streets in the centre of town. The owner comes in one morning and notices these bullet holes in the wall. He swears they weren't there the day before, so we interview the young lady who worked the night shift, and she swears she doesn't know how they got there. Now, the thing is, when we went to interview her, she had just quit her job at the restaurant—she gave her notice the very day that the owner came to see me about those bullet holes. And they were bullet holes—we dug the bullets out of the wall. Anyway, this young woman, she was pretty uncomfortable when we interviewed her. I don't think she's the one who shot those holes in the wall—what possible reason could she have for doing something like that? So, we're looking for witnesses who might have been in the area that night and might have heard something."

"Very odd."

"Say, that's the night we picked you up. You didn't happen to be near that restaurant during your wanderings, did you?"

"I can't say for sure, given what I remember of that night. Any odd goings-on concerned only myself."

"This young woman, she's a student at the university. Who knows, maybe you had her in one of your classes. April Bennett. Ring any bells?"

"Afraid not."

"Pretty thing. Not that I look any more, but you know."

"I'm not sure I'll ever know."

"Yeah, well I guess you've seen your share of pretty young women, given your occupation. Well, I'm turning down this street here. Maybe I'll see you around. Maybe in the middle of Charter Street one night."

‡

"The usual, dear?"

Sometimes it just feels good to be called 'dear.' Sometimes cinnamon toast and coffee is the best a man can hope for in a difficult world.

"Luella," I said, as she placed the toast and coffee on the table before me, "have you always lived here?"

"I'm a prairie girl."

It had been a long time since Luella was a girl.

"Why did you come here?"

"Got married before I knew what was good for me and followed my husband out near here."

"Still married?"

"There are some things you try once and then decide it's best not to do again."

She was off to get the next order from the kitchen, leaving me to wonder if she meant that she was still married, unhappily, it would seem, or if she had packed it in and was now a card-carrying single woman. I had to wait until she came by to refill my coffee before I could continue my probe.

"You still married, Luella?"

"Lord, no."

"Kids?"

"Sure," she said, waving her free arm down the aisle of booths.

"I hear you."

"Not everyone listens."

And she was off to pick up another order. I lazed my way through my second cup of coffee, looking idly around me at the faces of young students in between classes or skipping classes, catching snippets of musings about new courses, new professors and old professors, young men and women they were newly attracted to or still attracted to from last year; pausing on this face or that face, trying to imagine the uneasy mix of mild trepidation and major excitement roiling around in their brains caught somewhere between adolescence and adulthood. There were a couple of professor types, too, but I was the oldest person in the diner, except for Luella, who was around the same age I was, but wrinkled with different experiences from mine. I was relieved to no longer be in the classroom, on either side of the desk, but the long teeth of memory gnawed at my brain and heart. I could remember what it felt like to be those students seated all around me, but they could not, nor did they have any need to, project themselves forty years into the future and see things from my perspective. What would Esther make of these young minds and hearts and bodies? Would she sit beside me, a bridge between their wonder and my sorrow? Would she really find me?

"Hey, Professor Pepperfield, I heard you had retired. I'm sorry to see you go. I liked your courses a lot."

"Jeremy, how are you?"

I had had Jeremy in a first-year literature survey course and then again in my fourth year Twentieth Century American Poetry class. A boy/man trying to navigate a body that had grown too quickly in a vertical direction for the horizontal proportions to regulate themselves, he was one of the few bright male students to pass through my courses. Undergraduate literature courses were populated mostly by young women, and too many of the men who took these courses were too theoretically minded. The women could still connect heart with head, while the men were imprisoned in their minds, thinking they had chosen to be that way. I remembered Jeremy because he understood that the study of literature without any connection to the heart was simply unthinkable. He sat down across from me in my booth without considering the need to wait for an invitation.

"Shouldn't you be graduated by now?" I asked.

"I did get my English degree. Now I'm back picking up some extra courses so I can do graduate work in Religious Studies."

An obvious progression, I thought. I had always believed, and taught my courses on the, to me, natural assumption that the proper study of literature necessarily wandered through the foothills of religion, philosophy, mythology, psychology, anthropology, sociology—all the various disciplines in the Humanities and Social Sciences.

"Listen, can I pick your brain about something? There's this new prof for Twentieth Century Women's Poetry—she just arrived from England—the course was on the books, but they let us know that she wouldn't be here for the first week or two of classes—anyway, I signed up for it, but I'm wondering if you know anything about her, even though she's not from this side of the ocean. Her name is Professor Greenwood."

I had inserted my finger in the handle of my coffee cup, about to lift it from the saucer—that was another thing I loved about this diner—they still used cups and saucers—but set the cup back down in the saucer as carefully as I could, pretending nonchalance.

"Professor Greenwood?"

"Yeah, have you heard of her?"

"Professor Esther Greenwood?"

"I don't know her first name. She's written a couple of books on Edna St. Vincent Millay and Gwendolyn MacEwen."

"The name sounds familiar, but I'd have to do some checking."

I don't remember the rest of our conversation. I do remember rushing home to my computer and trying to control my fingers enough to search for Professor Esther Greenwood. She had graduated from Harvard and Cambridge and had been teaching various places in England since the sixties. I clicked on Images to see if I could find photographs of her. I did. She was fifty years older, but it was her. It was her! Why would a seventy-something-year-old English professor suddenly uproot herself from England to come across the ocean to teach at a new university? Why was she still teaching? Why would Riverdene hire a seventy-year-old professor of any gender from any country to join the English Department when she was long past retirement age? And how—HOW—could it be her?

I picked up my jacket from where I had thrown it on the floor and started to wrestle it on as I ran out of the house. I pushed through the front door, not caring if it shut properly behind me, took two long strides across the porch, and promptly tripped on the first step and collapsed in a forward moving heap on to the cement path at the bottom of the steps. My left leg, it if was not broken, was sending pain signals to my brain arguing that it was. There was blood seeping into the torn fabric of my jeans at the bend of my knee. I took a few minutes to let the pain subside from excruciating to merely nauseating before I gathered myself into a semblance of standing position. From there I hobbled over to my car, which I rarely ever drove because I preferred walking and because it was a 1967 Volkswagen bug that protested my involvement in its life whenever I was so thoughtless as to put the key in the ignition and turn it. But I was in a hurry and I was not in walking condition.

On the university grounds, I parked as close as I could, without risking a parking ticket, to the great limestone edifice at the top of the hill that housed the English Department. That still left me with a good couple of hundred yards to manoeuver my body towards and finally into the building.

"Professor Pepperfield," gushed Linda, the long-suffering secretary of the English Department, "how nice to see you. Enjoying your retirement?"

When she saw my bloody pant leg, she wished she'd asked a different question.

"Good lord, are you alright?"

"Just a flesh wound. Can you tell me what office Professor Greenwood's is in?"

"Funny you should ask that," said Linda, trying to substitute breeziness for concern. "She's in your old office."

Of course she was. I limped down the hallway I had walked several thousand times over the years, arriving at my old office out of breath and still in too much pain to be doing what I was doing. I knocked at the door.

"Come."

How British of her, I thought. I opened the door, stepped inside, and closed the door behind me.

"A wounded and dying soldier, indeed," she said, rising from my old chair behind my old desk. "It's been a long time."

"It was just a couple of days ago."

"Does it look like it was just a couple of days ago?" she asked, spreading her arms out as if she were a display model. "Different worlds, Levi. I think you need to sit down."

I did, but not because of my leg. Because of my fractured mind. She sat down in a chair next to me and put her hand on my arm. Seventy-something-year-old Esther Greenwood was a fully ripened version of the twenty-year-old Esther Greenwood I had left only a couple of days before. My mind tried its best to telescope fifty years of her life into the few minutes I sat there staring at her like some kid whose sense of time had been exploded, sucking the wind out of his body. Her beauty was a seasoned one; one that I knew I did not possess. And then, of course, there was the fact of my being in my old office, which, though it recognized me, held me at a distance.

"I had to catch up to you," she said. "There was no other way to do it. But I did tell you I'd find you."

"I don't know what to say. Even if I did, I wouldn't know how to say it. We've met, but we've never met."

"So, let us get acquainted."

"We can hardly just be acquaintances."

"Then let us exchange wounds once again. I see you've come with a much too literal one. Wait here."

She left the office and returned minutes later with a first-aid kit. She put it on the desk, opened it, and kneeled before me, my blood-soaked jeans down around my ankles. With the deftness of one who had treated such wounds many times before, she cleaned and bound the wound with a long strip of gauze, which she wound around my knee and then taped in place.

"The pants will require a nurse of a different kind," she said, as I struggled to pull them back up while still sitting down, "though I doubt the possibility of their resurrection."

She sat back on the chair next to mine.

"Would you like the *Readers Digest* version of my life since I last saw you?"

She explained to me the irony of relocating to England, a simple matter of remaining where she was after completing her graduate work at Cambridge, to specialize in the poetry of North American women. The discovery of tortured love in the poetry of Edna St. Vincent Millay, and later of the labyrinths of the renegade mind in the poetry of Gwendolyn MacEwen. Living male poets she had seduced and been seduced by, none of them able to coordinate the beauty of their words with the truth of who they were. The visits home that began as twice a year and dwindled slowly to once a year, to once every two years, to sporadic, to none at all for the past twenty-five years before coming here to Riverdene. The sorrow of having to let me go, a sorrow that, over the years, relaxed into wistfulness and then revived itself as anticipation as the time grew closer to coming to find me. The poems that measured her life into bowls of cut flowers whose beauty had to be renewed over and over again until renewal became a constant way of being; poems that she bound into packets tied together with string as Emily Dickinson had done. The students, especially the young women, in whom she kept her own young self alive. The geography of English moors, Scottish braes, Welsh mountains, all of which reconfigured her own spiritual geography. The discovery and acquisition of one of the ten remaining copies of the original 1846 Aylott and Jones publication of *Poems by Currer, Ellis, and Acton Bell*. The fortuitous conjunction of menopause with the realization that she was satisfied to never have had children. The sabbatical year she rented and lived on a canal boat and explored the pastoral waterways of England while writing a novel about a woman who falls in love with a time-travelling soldier, which she has not and never intends to publish. The letters she wrote me and kept in a shoebox in her bedroom closet, a journal of growing into and out of middle age. The embracing of the autumn of her life, like catching a fire-bright leaf as it drifted from the branch of a wise old maple tree in a forest in Dorset. Falling to her knees as she said goodbye to her thatch-roofed cottage in the village she had learned to call home for as long as she could.

"And now I'm here."

"What do we do now?"

‡

There are times when a man must sit back and reevaluate his life, but I have never been satisfied with the limitations of simple reevaluation. I immediately take out my blue pencil, as any normal editor would do. If life must be an exercise in losing what you do not wish to lose, if the number of possibilities for future accomplishment diminishes with each passing decade, then each passing year, then each passing month, like leafing through a manuscript of a determined length, then I think I should preserve the right to edit what is already on the page. But what happens when other stories—other worlds—have insinuated themselves into mine like smoke into a room where the windows have been painted shut and the door has been locked from the outside?

"What do we do now?" I asked Deborah later that evening.

She had brought some Bailey's to invigorate the coffee, and we sat on opposite ends of the sofa in my living room, legs stretched out towards and intertwined with each other's. I was thankful to still feel familiar with her; thankful, also, that she seemed to feel the same. I posed the question after she had shared her voyage into and out of *Now, Voyager*, after she had explained how she was able to send me letters between worlds.

"Enjoy the beauty of it all. Isn't that the truth behind what you've always wanted to do? Isn't that what you've spent your whole life trying to do?"

"You think it's that simple?"

"Who said it was simple? It is, though, the only thing you can do. You don't know how to do anything else."

"Predestination."

"Essence. First comes beauty, then comes goodness. An attentive reading of Genesis will tell you that when he created Eden, 'from the ground the Lord God caused to grow every tree that was pleasing to the sight and good for food.' Notice that beauty comes before goodness. The point is that anything that was beautiful was automatically good. It's not until Eve and Adam eat from the tree of knowledge of good and bad that beauty becomes separated from the good. But even then, that separation is a deception. Besides, we already know about each other, Esther and I. To try to separate us would only be a deception on your part."

"I think I need to reconfigure my coordinates, which I'm no longer sure I ever understood in the first place."

"Fine. In the meantime, would you care to reconfigure my coordinates? I brought cigarettes."

‡

Esther's answer to my question, "What do we do now?" had been as frustratingly simple as Deborah's.

"You take me to the diner for cinnamon toast tomorrow," she said, the hand she had placed on my arm giving it a little squeeze.

Her fingers pressed into my arm, not from forced pressure on her part, but from the simple gravitational pull of the blood pumping through my basilic vein. When she took her hand away, when she stood up from her chair, when I left my old office with her standing in it, that gravitational pull did not dissipate. I felt it all the way home. I felt it all during my conversation with Deborah, and I felt it even as I made love to her. It somehow lent itself to the passion that we gave ourselves up to, knowing that whatever lay on the far side of the evening had its own gravitational pull that could not be resisted.

We lay in bed, smoking our cigarettes, spent and sweaty and satisfied. Words, at that point, could not hold their own against all that was unspoken. They were perfunctory at best, and we were fine with that.

"Not a good idea for me to stay the night," said Deborah as a matter of observation rather than judgment. "Enjoy your cinnamon toast date tomorrow."

Esther had arrived at the diner before me. She was nursing a cup of coffee and reading the *Collected Poems of Edna St. Vincent Millay*. She looked up as I slid myself into the booth.

> "'My spirit, sore from marching
> Toward that receding west
> Where Pity shall be governor,
> With Wisdom for his guest.'

"Perhaps it is better to be sore than wounded," she said, smiling over the top of her cup as she raised it to her lips.

"There being no wisdom in being wounded?"

"A different wisdom, perhaps. Shall we order?"

At that moment, Luella stopped at our booth.

"The regular, dear?"

"Two orders, please, Luella."

"I'm Esther," said Esther, reaching her hand out to Luella.

"Pleased to meet you," said Luella, shaking Esther's offered hand. "You're always welcome here, especially in the company of Professor Pepperfield."

"I think you can call me Levi now."

"Why fix something if it ain't broke?" she smiled with her own subtle wisdom.

"She called you 'dear.'"

"She calls everyone 'dear.'"

"Fall is in the air. I missed that on the other side of the pond."

"You don't get autumn in England?"

"There isn't the clean crispness that you can feel here. I feel rather cleanly crisp myself. That feeling of being born yet again. Isn't September always like that for those of us who measure the year in semesters?"

"Or in worlds."

"How many other people, do you think, would understand who we are to each other?"

"Does it matter?"

"Do I detect a note of cynicism? And so early in the conversation."

"I'm sorry. I'm feeling a little out of time."

"In both senses of that statement? Yes, of course," she said, without waiting for my answer, "though you were probably conscious of only one sense when you said it. May I read you another passage from Millay's poem?"

Again, she continued without waiting for my response.

> "'Draw from the shapeless moment
> Such pattern as you can;
> And cleave henceforth to Beauty;
> Expect no more from man.'

"All those important words—pity, wisdom, beauty—are capitalized in the poem. I wonder why it was that poets forgot how to do that in their poetry. Perhaps they thought that we would know where the capitals were meant to go. I suppose that may have been true once, but not anymore. I think, though, that I would have capitalized 'pattern' as well. That's what we are—patterns. Intersecting patterns. That's where the beauty happens. And the truth. Patterns—that's what Keats saw on that Grecian urn."

"I fart and my shit smells."

I don't know why I said it; the words snuck out of my mouth while I was thinking what to do with my tongue.

"The attempt to describe life without idealization or romantic subjectivity. Keats would not have been amused."

"I just wanted to give you another perspective on me."

"Turning the kaleidoscope?"

"Bringing it back to default setting."

"Do you really expect me to set aside everything I know about you, everything I've experienced with you because you fart and your shit smells, or because you have the boldness, or whatever you think it is, to say the words out loud in my presence?"

The cinnamon toast arrived. Luella placed the two plates in front of us, then quickly eyed each of us. She paused a bit longer on Esther.

"She's new here. You treat her nice," she said to me.

"Not who I pictured as my knight in shining armour," said Esther.

"You hardly need a knight these days."

"These days?"

"You're not who you used to be."

"And how would you know that?"

"I've read your resumé."

"And you really believe that defines who I am?"

"Let's just say that you couldn't have reached the heights you have if you still needed a knight in shining armour to protect you."

"You're so very wrong about that. We all need a knight in shining armour, or any kind of armour at all. Maybe even no armour at all. Just fortitude and compassion. Why do you feel you need to deny my vulnerability?"

I wanted to reach my hand across the table and touch her; I wanted to remind myself of the gravitational pull. I wanted to apologize. Instead, I tried to fortify myself with a bite of cinnamon toast.

"It really is good cinnamon toast," she said.

There was a relief in her voice that might have been because she had been worried the toast would not live up to the expectations I had set, or because the toast was just a safe space for us both to retreat to for the moment.

"And there is no default setting on a kaleidoscope," she said. "However, we can talk about essence, if you'd like."

And so, we did. We talked of Grecian urns and kaleidoscopes, of quantum mechanics and the "Intimations of Immortality," of five-year-old selves and sixty- and seventy-year-old selves, of whether existence preceded essence, of students becoming teachers becoming students—the circle of the learned and learn'd life. As we parted and promised to meet again sometime during the week, she hugged me (and yes, I will admit to a moderate sexual arousal), and offered, "How about 'I am gaseous and excretionally scented.'"

‡

I needed to reacquaint myself with my particular place and time, to reorient myself to the ground on which I had been standing for much of my life before the trajectory of my desire intersected with that of Esther Greenwood. To that end, when I left Esther after our cinnamon toast meeting at the diner, I went walking along the river, a walk I had taken hundreds of times during my years as a student and a professor at Riverdene. I was continually surprised that more people didn't take that walk. I expected, on every walk I took, that I would meet at least one or two other people, or, more likely, several the longer my walk, but far more often than not I found myself alone, which was my preference anyway.

The path along the river was taking on its annual crinkly autumnal cushion of fallen leaves, so that my feet made a dry swishing sound with each step. The smell of freshly dead leaves was a gift my nose waited for all year. I wished that my life were a natural cycle; I wished that instead of marching inexorably towards death, never to return, I could keep circling back to experience all the seasons of my life over and over again. It was not Nietzche's horrifyingly paralytic concept of eternal recurrence, but Heine's eternal return that appealed to me: "For time is infinite, but the things in time, the concrete bodies are finite. . . . Now, however long a time may pass, according to the eternal laws governing the combinations of this eternal play of repetition, all configurations that have previously existed on this earth must yet meet, attract, repulse, kiss, and corrupt each other again. . . . And thus it will happen one day that a man will be born again, just like me." I would have preferred, of course, that one day "a man will be born again, who *is* me."

As I reached the far end of my walk, somewhere past the boundary of the university campus, I came upon a young man and woman embracing, kissing. I stood back so as not to interrupt them, staying just out of sight so that I could observe them. I do not consider myself to be a voyeur; in that moment, rather, I simply wanted to witness something pure. The kiss was clearly either their first or very near to the first. It was slow and measured; they were like two people who had crossed a desert in search of water and knew well enough when they found it to take slow draughts lest they make themselves sick. I felt a catch of breath, a minor constriction of the chest, a sudden delicious sorrow. If I were a sorcerer or a wizard, I would have cast a spell on them so that they could live in this moment forever.

I returned home and put on a record of the Goldberg Variations. I liked to see how long I could follow all the voices at the same time. I have yet to manage this focus for the entire theme and thirty variations, and trying to do so is one of the pleasures of indulging in this piece. I also find it pleasurable to know that this is the only time Bach ever composed variations and that they were composed specifically for a two-manual harpsichord, and that the recording I had was the first ever made of the Goldberg Variations—Wanda Landowska in 1933 on a two-manual harpsichord. I wondered if Trisha Brewster played the Variations.

‡

Sometimes days pass and you can't remember what you did with them, an extended version of driving home from work and pulling into your driveway, reeling your mind in from whatever daydream it had been lost in and wondering how it was you managed to drive home without having been conscious of driving—how was it that you didn't run a red light or fail to turn where you were supposed to or accelerate and brake at appropriate times, how it was that you didn't inadvertently kill or maim some innocent person along the way? For those few days, I'm sure I didn't see Esther or Deborah or Violet—I would have remembered those encounters.

I was sitting on the porch, as I so often do—I often think my life these days has been lived on this porch, with sporadic forays into the world beyond the steps that lead down from the porch. As I was sitting there on this day, I had to wonder how long—not hours, but days and nights—I'd been gently rocking in the swing chair. I didn't see her come up the walk or up the stairs to the porch; I didn't recall her sitting down in the swing chair beside me, but there she was, as if she'd always been there.

"I finished my assignment," Violet said, handing me a large manila envelope with my name handwritten on the outside.

I must have been staring at her with a confused look on my face.

"The assignment? The one about Corinthians? The letter I wrote you from Corinth?" she prodded.

"Of course."

I turned the envelope around in my hand. It was too thin to have the bulk of a printed assignment inside it; it felt empty. I opened it. It was, indeed, empty. I splayed my hands, the empty envelope in one hand, the other hand empty of my coffee cup.

"Well?" I said.

"What was that experience like?" she asked.

"What experience?"

"The one of having an expectation and then having it deflected."

"Deflected?"

"Deflected. Not met or unmet, just deflected. Set off on a trajectory not included in the possible responses you expected to have."

"And were you deflected from completing the assignment?"

"I did complete it. I dug below the surface to find truth and beauty, just as you told me to do."

"And you found it?"

"I found where truth and beauty come from."

She sat back in the swing chair as if she'd just made an obvious conclusion, which did not require any further explanation.

"And?"

"They come from here," she said, sticking out her tongue and tapping it with her finger. "Literally, metaphorically, sexually—they come from here," she said, her tongue having retreated into her mouth. "The sound, the words, the arousal—they all come from here," she expanded, sticking out her tongue again and tapping it with her finger again. "The sound the human voice makes is the truth of sorrow, just as the sound the rain makes is the truth of the clouds. All these words are the truth of emotions and intellect. When tongues touch each other or some part of another's body—that's the truth that precedes and surpasses all other truths."

"And beauty?"

"Beauty is knowing all those truths."

"And you discovered all this by going to first century Corinth?"

The question was not meant to be sarcastic or even ironic; I was truly curious. She had leaped beyond the bounds of the assignment as I had structured it in my mind. This was probably a good thing, but I will admit to feeling a certain sense of having been superseded as a professor—as her professor. I still needed to be a teacher in the eyes, and yes, I suppose, on the tongue, of my students, who would always be my students no matter how much wisdom they accumulated beyond their time with me.

"I went to first century Corinth because you gave me an assignment, which was to read First Corinthians chapter fourteen. I got that assignment because I decided to come to your house and give you a chance at resurrection. I came to your house because I met you serendipitously at a bar one night and sat down to have a drink with you. I had a drink with you because I was in your class. I was in your class because I decided to be a literature major. I decided to be a literature major because I liked reading books. I liked reading books because it was the only place available to me where I could find people who didn't make me think I was crazy. I thought I was crazy because the world made sense to me in ways I couldn't explain to anyone else. I couldn't explain the way I understood the world to anyone else because the language everybody used wasn't my language. I was speaking in tongues, and nobody could understand me. Until I was in your class, until I read *Franny and Zooey*, I had been programmed to believe that prophecy, the language of one mind speaking to other minds, was better than speaking in tongues, the language that depended on mystery. Truth is mysterious; beauty is the glow of that mystery. A good teacher is a teacher who speaks in tongues. A good teacher challenges his students to learn how to interpret tongues by figuring out that when they are true to themselves they are necessarily speaking in tongues themselves. If the majority of the students in a class don't get that, it's their problem, not the teacher's. Just because you're no longer in front of a class doesn't mean you have to stop speaking in tongues. Consider yourself deflected."

She leaned over and kissed me on the cheek. I swear I could feel the tip of her tongue flick my cheek. She stood up abruptly, setting the swing chair into motion, and walked down the steps from the porch, walked down the path to the road, walked down that road until I couldn't see her walking anymore. Somehow it was evening and the moon was rising above the trees at the end of the road.

‡

An Aside . . .

"LET ME BE a seal upon your heart"—Deborah prefers this translation to "Set me as a seal upon your heart"—these words ask permission rather than demand the action. "Like the seal upon your arm"—is this where the expression "wear your heart on your sleeve" comes from? Seal—not just some random mark, but a seal, a sign of intimate connection and identity: I can identify you; you can identify me; we can identify love—fierce love. "For love is fierce as death"—all the standard translations say "For love is strong as death," but *az* means "fierce" as well as "strong." She likes the extra edge of that particular adjective, especially when it is a consequence of asking rather than demanding.

Tonight, Deborah reads The Song of Songs, which she often does when she tries to determine her connection with Levi. She reads the meaning of the Song as *nigleh* rather than *nistar*: apparent or revealed rather than hidden. She does not understand The Song of Songs as a dialogue between God and Israel or between God and the Soul, or between the Torah and its disciples or as between the feminine and masculine aspects of divinity—there is divinity, to be sure, but it is the divinity of human love, which is a mirror of the divine love between God and his creation. She knows The Song of Songs is a love story, a story of passion and the anticipation of passion.

In the midst of The High Holy Days she smokes a cigarette and drinks a glass of wine and looks for answers where she has yet to clearly articulate the questions. This is what is left of her secular self, the self that comes knocking at her door when she is too tired to be a rabbi, even too tired to be a good practicing Jew. So, she pays more careful attention on these days to her *Shema*, which she chants first thing in the morning when she wakes and last thing before she goes to bed. During Rosh Hashanah she devotes more time than usual to *Kavanah*, that high state of focused attention, emptied of thought and emotion.

Tonight, she chants her *Shema*, then releases herself to *Kavanah*. She goes to bed and falls into a deep, dreamless sleep. A respite.

☦

Violet walks down the road away from Professor Pepperfield's porch, vibrating towards the rising moon, her feet trying to remember the rhythm they learned in her journey from Seleucia to Magdala. To walk to, to walk from; to walk to and fro. There, she walked the moon into and out of fullness, beginning and ending in moonlessness. There, she was a long string, tuned to a lower pitch, vibrating in long, slow waves when plucked. Here, the string is shorter, tauter, vibrating in shorter, more excited waves when plucked. There, she was plucked by time. Here, she is plucked by Professor Pepperfield.

She follows her feet to the bar where she orders a martini and sits at the table where she sat with Professor Pepperfield. She allows a young man who seems vaguely familiar—perhaps they were in the same class in some past semester—to sit at the table with her. He is drinking beer from a bottle. He is a Business major. He is looking to "party." He asks if he can buy her another drink. He does not know how to speak in tongues. She thanks him for his offer, declines it, and leaves because he does not understand that he should leave, instead.

Violet follows her feet to the cathedral. There are more and wider steps than those up to Professor Pepperfield's porch. The carved stone structure rises above her, makes her feel too small to move. It takes her an unmeasurable amount of time to arrive at the vast wooden doors, to pull them open, to stand at the beginning of the aisle that telescopes into the altar at the far end of the yawning space. What would Chloe and Phoebe and Priscilla and Junia make of such a structure? And Thecla? Mary? Could she, Violet Trevelyan, connect Corinth to the Four Quartets? "I like the kind of Christian Eliot is," she had told Professor Pepperfield. "A poetic Christian. A Christian who understands metaphor." This is the kind of Christian who leaves something beautiful behind, even if the source of the metaphor gets locked inside airless glass cases where it can only suffocate. Violet understands that Professor Pepperfield has left something beautiful behind in her, but that he either does not know it or refuses to acknowledge it. She has been seeded. Not the violent biological seed that a man leaves inside a woman—that is a gross affair; that is not the seed she wants left inside her. To speak in tongues is to seed the imagination with mystery, with desire, with transcendence. That is how she has been seeded by Professor Pepperfield. That is how she wants to seed the world.

The vast, empty space of the cathedral thunders with silence. "Let your women keep silence in the churches; for it is not permitted unto them to speak"—so says Paul. Violet will keep her silence, for silence is the tongue in the bell waiting for someone who knows how to ring it.

‡

Dr. E. Greenwood. The nameplate on the door replaces Dr. L. Pepperfield. Whenever she walks into her office, Esther walks into the temple of Levi Pepperfield's past. He has left behind him a silence that echoes off the book lined walls like the words of prophets whose voices have retreated into the distance of time. The shelves of his chosen, bound words have now been replaced with her own. They are all the same words, just differently configured. She remembers configurations of her old self, catching sight of the proverbially perfect man in the distance and then discarding the possibility of him as soon as he moved closer. She has collapsed the distance between herself and Levi, but has preserved the quality of it, as one must. For she also remembers that she did not want to be the arrow that someone else shot; she wanted to shoot off in all directions herself, like the coloured arrows from a Fourth of July rocket, her own vehicle of change and excitement. Her arc has been a long one, and as she slowly descends towards the ground she has gathered enough years to regret none of them. Like the fall, she will burn with cool fire, lighting up the ever-shortening days with the seeds of wisdom.

Today, she is preparing a class on Edna St. Vincent Millay's poem "Departure":

> "'I wish I could walk for a day and a night,
> And find me at dawn in a desolate place
> With never the rut of a road in sight,
> Nor the roof of a house, nor the eyes of a face.'"

It is the second line that she wants her students to pay close attention to— "find me," as if she had found some object that had long lain abandoned or undiscovered, in a place where there are no reference points and no witnesses. This sounds like arrival, not departure. The question, then, is: can there be one without the other, no matter which of the two you begin with.

> "'I wish I could walk till my blood should spout,
> And drop me, never to stir again,
> On a shore that is wide, for the tide is out,
> And the weedy rocks are bare to the rain.'"

To be dropped by your own blood—what is departing from what? To exchange the ocean for the rain—eternal vastness for the temporary shower or storm. Sometimes not even the poet is aware of her own wisdom—who gives her such words that she feed the hungry and starve herself?

And A Return . . .

It has been too long since I sat down and tried to write a poem; rather, it has been too long since I was able to take an idea from among the pages of penciled bits of thought I keep in the pocket-sized notebook I carry around with me and flesh it out, give it muscle and sinew, tendon and ligament to hold it all together, to give it flexibility and structure at the same time. "Too long" is too vague. Twenty years is more precise. I have lived a life of fragments since then:

> "we want to be ancient, to be elemental; we want to no longer be abandoned . . ."
> "the intermittent moan of foghorns pokes holes in the dark soil of sleep where dreams drip their seed . . ."
> "today I am too tender for the talk of human words; I have been bruised by their indifference, sapped by their incessance . . ."
> "to the stoic silence of stones do we trust our history, do we hope our borrowed names to be remembered onto the lips of the curious . . ."
> "sometimes the grass and pines are their own words; they speak themselves in green textures, in quotations of sun and moon . . ."
> "we have created words to love ourselves with, but in the confusion of grammar have pressed our eyes into hard round stones that roll down empty streets with our names on every corner . . ."
> "it is time for saying what we need to say, for opening fists into hands and letting promises find their ground . . ."

"we live a history of forgetfulness, destined to
be remembered for what we did not leave
behind . . ."

My last completed poem, an afterthought attached to all the poems that came before it, a door closing on the silence in the next room:

> From opposite sides
> of the train window we are
> balanced on the edge
> of separation. The glass
>
> uncouples voice
> from gesture. We are
> disarticulated. You
>
> are frozen on the receding
> platform, guarding the negative
> inside the camera in which
>
> I have never been allowed
> to leave the station,
>
> in which I have forever
> surrendered impetus
> to implication.

I wrote that poem for a woman I didn't even know. The train was pulling out of the station with me in it, and she was standing on the platform, left behind by someone on the same train. I remember that she was beautiful in that way that women who have given their hearts away and are helpless to recognize the sorrow of their loss are beautiful. I imagined that she was looking at me, that we had been in love, and that something had caused me to leave without her, even though she wanted to come with me. Even before that time, and especially since that time, I have become a connoisseur of sorrow, sipping it slowly, swirling it around in my mouth, letting the quick bite soften into slow flame before swallowing it into the centre of my being.

I went to my desk, opened the drawer to find a pencil, opened the large notebook that wondered who I was. I opened all the channels I could remember, prostrating myself on the long-forgotten altar. "Just give me somewhere to start," I said into the nothingness. Deborah. An image of my tongue sliding down from her neck, stuttering on the hardness of her nipples . . .

The phone rang. The channels closed themselves off, having no patience for someone who could not at least find a quiet place in which to not be disturbed while seeking a poem.

"Hello," I said, my voice unable to unplug my frustration, not only because I'd been interrupted, but because I didn't have the discipline to unplug the phone instead of answering it.

"Is this 822-0575?"

"Yes."

"You gave me your number at the speed dating night last week. Is this a bad time?"

Of course it was a bad time.

"Not at all."

"You sound as if I've taken you away from something."

"I'm not good at answering phones. It always takes me more than one word to warm up. I'm surprised you called."

It was only last week? Time had decided to rearrange all its facial features so that I could stare it right in the face and not recognize it.

"I'm kind of surprised, too. Would you like to go out for a drink sometime? If you drink, that is. If you don't we could just grab a coffee."

"I think alcohol would be the correct beverage in this situation."

"That's what I was thinking. By the way, we never got each other's names. My name is Angela."

"Levi," I said. "Where would you like to meet?"

"There's a pub on Charter downtown—The Churchill."

That was the pub in which I'd run across my former students, the one in which Violet and I sat down to have a drink, the one in which I proceeded to be a bit of an asshole.

"Is tonight too soon?" she asked.

It was.

"Sounds good. Eight o'clock?"

☦

"You do have normal clothes," she said, after having waved to me from a table in the middle of the room. "I'm relieved."

I hated sitting in the middle of a room, whether it was a classroom when I was a student, or a restaurant, or a movie theatre, in which my seat against the right or left-hand wall allowed for privacy but not for the ultimate viewing experience. Whenever I had to sit in the middle of a room, I was sure everyone else in the room was staring at me instead of taking notes, conversing with their dinner companion, or staring at the screen.

"I hope you don't mind sitting in the middle of the room," she said.

"Not at all."

She was wearing, as far as I could remember, the very same outfit she wore on the speed dating night.

"Yes, it's the same outfit. I wanted you to be able to recognize me. I didn't know if I would recognize you in normal clothes, so I got here a half hour early to allow you to find me if I couldn't find you."

The waitress brought my Jameson and her Blind Russian. Again, I was studying too hard.

"It's like a White Russian, with vodka and Kahlua, but Bailey's Irish Cream instead of regular cream. My father is Russian, my mother Irish. Silly, I know."

"You like your parents?"

"They're both dead, but yes, I did like them. You?"

"My parents were non-descript. Both dead, too."

Even though she leaned more towards the beautiful than the ordinary, I was not as immediately stimulated as I wanted to be.

I compared her breasts, what I could see of them under her loose-fitting sweater top, with Deborah's, whose breasts commanded the eyes, no matter what she wore; I compared her eyes, which were a kind of hazel colour, with Esther's, a deep brown like chestnuts just fallen and cracked open, inviting my own eyes to try to gleam like them; I compared her hands with Violet's—I haven't yet described Violet's hands, those hands that I first paid attention to when we had a drink together in this very pub, as they massaged her martini glass. Her fingers were long, with a kind of muted elegance—no nail polish to distract the eye from wandering over the whole hand. Angela had blood red fingernails, cut very short. A man has too many women in his life when he helplessly indulges in these kinds of comparisons. Give her a chance, I said to myself.

"What do you do?" she asked me.

I explained my academic career and recent retirement, tossing in the names of some of my favourite writers.

"You?" I asked.

"A lawyer."

"I didn't expect that."

"What were you expecting?"

There was an edge to her question.

"I don't know what I was expecting."

"You were obviously expecting something, because my being a lawyer was not what you were expecting."

"I thought a lawyer would be more, I don't know, forceful."

"Do you listen to jazz?"

"Not that much."

"You should. There's a saxophonist named David Sanborn—he plays some jazz, some rock 'n roll, some R&B, but he's always tuned in to all the other instruments he plays with. For instance, he said that, and I quote, 'when you have an acoustic bass in the ensemble it really changes the dynamic of the record because it kind of forces everybody to play with a greater degree of sensitivity and nuance because it just has a different kind of tone and spectrum than the electric bass.' I'm an acoustic bass. I would think that as an English professor you would be more tuned into nuances."

"That was beautifully put."

"You're surprised."

"I just didn't expect . . ."

"You're not expecting much from me, are you? I know, you don't think I look and sound like a lawyer, though you're not sure what a female lawyer should look and sound like, and you think a lawyer wouldn't end up at a speed dating table, and maybe you even think I'm too attractive, in that intellectually challenged way, to be a lawyer. How am I doing so far?"

"Better than I . . ."

"Better than you expected? Really? Is that what you were going to say?"

It was, but not in the context in which she had framed it.

"And by the way, I could see you measuring me against every other woman you've been with. You're not very subtle."

"I was trying to give you a chance . . ." I began, but stopped, realizing I was carrying on a conversation that began in my own head rather than the one I was stumbling my way through with Angela. I was like a man digging a deep hole and who kept shouting out from below ground, "Hand me another shovel; the blade on this one is getting dull!"

"You know why I think you insisted on that opening line that you fart and your shit smells? Because you're an asshole."

She shoved her chair back from the table and just as abruptly got up and left. She took a few steps towards the door, stopped, whirled about, and came back to the table. She took a deep breath. Then she took a notebook out of her shoulder bag, scribbled something on it, tore it out, and handed it to me.

"Here's my phone number."

She paused for just a second, as if about to explain why she'd done what she just did, but for some reason I would never get to know, decided against it, turned away from me, and walked aggressively away.

I downed the rest of my Jameson and ordered another one. I wished Deborah were sitting across the table from me right now. Instead of replaying everything Angela had just said to me, all I could hear in my head was Deborah's voice. I remembered our conversation about when I was five years old and picking up a *klipah*. I took out my notebook. I flipped back through the pages, looking for the beginning bits of a poem that I might be able to consummate in my present condition, which, though I had tripped and fallen over my own social incompetence, was still supple enough with the right lubrication. I found a page from when I had gone back "home" to watch the sunrise from the top of the driveway of my old house and to unexpectedly find Mary. Something about being five years old; something about finding and losing myself.

> My five-year-old foot is held in a deep squelch
> of grabbing mud, my voice rolls through a silver
> tunnel narrowing up into a thin cup of moon.
> My fingers hang in the twists of bindweed
> holding the remains of a rail fence like the bones
> of an old dream that cannot settle into sleep.
> The skin of my knee is pressed into the dusty
> white bark of birches, their dull glow
> haunting the dark groves when I am not there.
> These are the pieces of me I visit when I go
> back home to the woods and the marsh and the creek;
> this is where I put myself together,
> where my blood is always bleeding.

I wrote the words. I read them back to myself. I read them out loud. Something to work with, I thought. Maybe another Jameson.

> My five-year-old foot squelches deep into
> the sucking mud. My voice calls through
> a silver tunnel, spilling into a thin cup of moon
> like a petition

No, best to leave this to a less sloppy mind. Just enjoy the Jameson and don't ask it to perform what it must surely believe is a stereotypical service to maudlin poets. Surely, the glasses and bottles of Jameson down through the years must have formed a union, with one of their founding constitutional principles being that they are tired to death of having to endure the drunken gush of slurred words onto notebook pages and napkins and coasters. "We want to be imbibed for our selves," they shout at their organizing meeting, "not as sloppy lubricant for questionable poetic talent, Brendan Behan aside. Taste us for our own unadulterated beauty, our own simple truth."

I am not a man who holds his liquor well. So, I ordered a fourth Jameson to prove my point.

"You sure you want this one?" asked the waitress, perhaps showing genuine concern.

"Are you genuinely concerned?" I asked her.

"I'm an experienced observer."

"I am no longer able to determine exactly what it is I want. However, I am immediately familiar with this Irish whiskey, and so one might say that I am sticking with what I know in the immediate situation. By the way, it might also interest you to know that I fart and my shit smells. I share this information with you because I believe that any relationship, however brief, should be based on those truths which are too seldom articulated."

"You look like a decent guy, and I want you to stay that way, so you're not getting another whiskey. The next time I see you in here I don't want to think to myself, 'Oh god, not that guy.' Don't be that guy. Can I call you a cab?"

"I surrender."

"Good choice."

When the cab dropped me off at home, I took out my wallet to pay the driver.

"Already paid for," he said.

"By whom?"

I could still control my objective pronouns no matter what other temporary infirmities I was suffering.

"The waitress at the pub. Said her sister took one of your courses a few years back. Said her sister said you were a good guy. Said you could pay her back next time you were in."

‡

I made it as far as the porch, where I rested before making a foray into the house to perk a pot of coffee, upon the completion of which I returned to the porch to bivouac. I wasn't totally convinced that I should disturb my Jameson buzz, but it was cold on the porch, and I wanted to have something to keep my hands, as well as my innards, warm. I also wanted to clear my mind just enough to try to assess my day. I wanted to figure out if the minor seisms of Violet's presentation of her completed assignment and Angela's rightful indignation concerning my social ineptitude might trigger any aftershocks—how many there might be and of what magnitude. But I was overtaken by the immediacy of my environment—the texture of darkness emphasized by the single streetlight on the far side of the road, by the dim porch light above my head, by the presence of a moon in transition, though it was hidden from me somewhere in the far periphery of my vision, horizoned as it was by tall trees and rooftops. The air, too, had its own texture—chill and thin and deliciously inspirable. For a few glorious moments, everything and everyone else, even all the versions of my self that I had constructed and sometimes forgotten, fell away. I experienced presentness. I had no history, no age—there was no such thing as context. If the phone rang, I did not hear it. If the world ended, I was not aware of it.

"Feels good, doesn't it?"

He was standing at the end of the walk in the pool of light from the streetlamp where the delta of the road and the rest of the neighbourhood spread away from it. He had his fishing rod in one hand, and the bounty of some river hanging on a string from the other. His face was hidden in the shadow of his floppy felt hat. I lifted my coffee cup to him as a silent toast. He lifted his string of fish in reply, then continued down the road until he bonded with the darkness.

"He kept moving in and out of the light, never able to understand what it was," said the white-bearded poet sitting on the top step of the porch. "Sometimes a man just has to stay still."

I lifted my coffee cup in a second silent toast. He responded with his cane, then set it back down on the ground, pushing himself up with its help. He moved in slow motion down the walk, paused when he got to the road, looked in the direction the fisherman had taken, and took the opposite route. I finished my cup of coffee, decamped from the porch, and set out for my bedroom.

‡

The morning after the night of Jameson. Another brand of clarity altogether. And another of those morning erections that men in their sixties are never sure what to do with, or why they persist at all. Walk it off, as my high school gym teacher would say when I tried, from a running start, to leap on to one end of the pommel horse unsuccessfully. A steady rain was doing its best to rid the trees of their remaining leaves, but it knew it would have to return later in the season to finish the job. It was a cinnamon toast morning.

"The usual, dear?"

"Make it a double, Luella."

"Are you ignoring her?"

"Ignoring whom?"

"That nice new professor I told you to be nice to. She's sitting just over there," she said, nodding her head down and across the aisle.

"I didn't know she was here."

"Maybe you want to do something about that."

"Thanks, Luella."

I had brought along *The Complete Poems and Plays* of T.S. Eliot. It felt like a J. Alfred Prufrock kind of day:

> "There will be time, there will be time
> To prepare a face to meet the faces that you meet."

"'Time for you and time for me,' said Esther, suddenly standing and reading over my shoulder, 'And time yet for a hundred indecisions, and for a hundred visions and revisions, before the taking of cinnamon toast and coffee,'" she revised the last line. "Luella told me you were here. She said she told you I was here, as well, but she didn't have much faith in your ability to do anything useful with the information. May I?" she asked, motioning to the bench on the opposite side of the booth.

"Day off?" I asked.

"It's Saturday, Levi."

"Every day is Saturday for those of the leisure class."

"If you'd read Veblen's Theory of the Leisure Class, you might choose a different stratus in which to place yourself."

I hadn't and I didn't care to pursue that line of conversation.

"Do you like Eliot?" I asked as a deflective response.

"Has a bit of a stick up his bottom, but does some lovely things with words."

I searched my brain for another deflection. Esther supplied her own.

"I have a very interesting student in my class. Violet Trevelyan."

"Does she know?"

"Not yet."

"Does she need to know?"

"I wouldn't steer the conversation in another direction if she managed to figure it out for herself."

"Have you spoken much with her?"

"An initial interview. I like to do that with all my students at the beginning of the semester. She is a woman beyond herself. Without a competent guide, she's in dangerous territory."

"Are you that guide?"

"I'm afraid she thinks you are. She didn't say it in so many words, but it seemed fairly clear to me."

"And you don't think I'm the right person for the job."

"Do you?"

"I have my moments."

"You're obviously impressed with her, and the feeling seems to be mutual, but she will soon ask you for something you won't be able to give her."

Time to deflect.

"I've been trying to write poetry again."

"A different road to danger."

"Have you been writing all these years?"

"I have."

"And?"

"The reviews and criticisms and books I toss into the wider world to see where they will land. The poems I keep to myself."

"I'd like to read them."

"I keep them to myself."

"Too dangerous to unleash on the world?"

"The world wouldn't think so."

"Fear, then?"

"When a knight prepares to joust, she does not first take off all her armour and drop her lance before spurring her steed into the contest."

"And you are the poem?"

She reached across the table and picked up a piece of cinnamon toast from my plate.

"So how do you explain," I continued, "all those poets who dare to publish their poetry? Are they on fools' errands?"

"You'd have to ask them."

"I'm asking you."

"Do you plan to publish your poetry?"

"Do I have to do all the heavy lifting in this conversation?" I asked with mild exasperation.

"You weren't so cantankerous when we first met."

"You weren't so evasive."

"Alright. Let me lay my cards on the table."

She shifted our cups and my plate to the side of the table.

"What kind of cards?" I asked. "Regular deck? Tarot? Runic?"

"You could try to meet me half way."

"Sorry."

"There was one more suicide attempt."

She stared hard into my eyes and locked me into position so I couldn't escape from what she said.

"I did publish one book of poetry. It was a few years after you left and I had completed my graduate work at Cambridge. The book appeared in Great Britain and I had landed a job teaching creative writing at a small university in the southeast. I got good reviews and was on the edge of celebrityhood, as far as a poet can be a celebrity. But I was young, I was quick, and I was attractive. It took me a long time to be able to use that last adjective on myself—long after the episode I'm going to tell you about. I thought I had a clear sense of myself after all I'd been through stateside. I was confident. I was in control of my life. But then, as I said, the book came out and there was a general consensus of acclaim. There was also an older Englishman who believed he had fallen in love with me simply by having read my poetry. He had never met me, never seen me—there wasn't even a photo of me on the dust jacket. I found out much later that he had declared to those who would listen that he was going to marry me. One day I answered a knock at my door, and there stood this man who proceeded to recite my own poetry to me. It was the look in his eyes that scared me. But it was more than that—as each word of my poem sounded into the space between us, it felt like some surgical tool assaulting me without anaesthetic. When he finished reciting my poem, he told me I was even more beautiful than my words. I felt that I'd been disemboweled and my guts were slopping out of me on to the ground. I summoned all the strength I had—physical, psychic, emotional—and pushed the door closed, using my last ounce of consciousness to lock it before collapsing to the floor.

"When I came to, I don't know how much later, I was terrified, not because of the man, but because of my reaction. It was out of all proportion to the act, creepy as it was. I went into the kitchen, closed the door behind me, and blew out the pilot flame of the gas stove and turned on all the jets to full open. But the smell of the gas made me sick. I was on the edge of passing out when I fell and hit my head on the edge of the table. It was enough to jolt me into what consciousness I had left. I stumbled out of the kitchen and out of my flat without turning the gas off.

I pounded on the door of the woman who lived next door. All I could say was "gas . . . stove . . . gas . . . stove." She called the fire brigade.

"Later, in her sitting room, I lied to the firemen that I couldn't get the stove to work—I had turned on all the jets but couldn't get a flame. They politely, but skeptically, explained that the pilot light had gone out and that was the problem. Long story short, I moved to another part of town and began to reassess my life as a poem. In the years since, and there have been, thankfully, many of them, I learned that poetry was a power I couldn't control. I can control other poets' poetry, I can open up to it, but I have to be careful with my own."

"There have been a lot of years since then."

"One must gather one's years carefully."

"Do you ever wish you could just revive the years you already have instead of gathering new ones?"

"Sit around and turn the pages of old photograph albums and yearbooks?" she said. "How does one die properly if they don't lay the table for the last guest?"

"I'd like to unfail failed moments."

"Once you lift your hand from the chess piece, you can't change your mind. Those are the rules."

I requested another double order of cinnamon toast from Luella, given that Esther had eaten half of my first order. We waited in silence for the toast to arrive. It reminded me of sitting in church waiting for the priest and altar boys to come out and begin the Mass.

"Do you know why Violet chose to take my course? She's intrigued by the personal madnesses of St. Vincent Millay and MacEwen. She told me in her interview that she wanted to trace the poetry back to the madness, then trace the madness to the poetry. She has this idea that madness is a consequence of speaking in tongues. I suppose she has you to thank for that. So, you see what I mean by danger."

"Not just for her, I presume."

"I have a comfortable agreement with danger. We respect each other enough not to wish to destroy the other."

"You said Violet needed a competent guide. Who was your guide?"

"Philomena Guinea. She donated the money for my college scholarship and paid for my time in the asylum. She was already elderly when I met her. She was a writer and had spent some time in an asylum when she was younger. She wrote a book about that experience."

"I suppose I could have used a guide, too."

"You had one."

"Not that I know of."

"Everyone has a guide," she argued. "The guide doesn't always show up at the same time for each person—could be when you're two years old, might not be till you're in your fifties or even later. It's just that too many of us aren't aware of the fact that we have a guide, whenever they show up.

"And if we aren't aware, then we don't benefit from having that guide?"

"Unfortunately, yes, that's how it is."

"Do you know who my guide was?"

"It doesn't matter if I know or not; it only matters if you know."

"Then it doesn't matter at all, because I don't know."

‡

"Yom Kippur begins at sunset tonight."

"Yom Kippur?"

"The Day of Atonement."

"Like Catholic confession?"

"Hardly. This only happens once a year. 'For on this day atonement shall be made for you to cleanse you of all your sins; you shall be clean before the Lord. It shall be a Sabbath of complete rest for you, and you shall practice self-denial; it is a law for all time'—Leviticus. So, no eating, no drinking, no bathing, no intimacy."

"No smoking of cigarettes?"

"No smoking of cigarettes. Rabbi Simeon ben Gamliel, though, said that Yom Kippur was the happiest day of the year for the people of Israel. The young girls of Jerusalem would dress all in white and venture forth to dance in the vineyards, singing 'Lift up your eyes, young man, and look around, that you might make your choice. Look not for beauty, but look for family.' And then he quoted the last verses of Proverbs: 'Grace is deceptive, Beauty is illusory, it is for her fear of the Lord that a woman is to be praised. Extol her for the fruit of her hand, and let her works praise her in the gates.'"

"I'm too big a fan of beauty, and not a great fan of family; I don't think I'd make a good Jew."

"Family doesn't mean just procreating. Two people can be a family."

"Do they have to be married?"

"Marriage can be interpreted in more than one way. Don't worry, Levi, I'm not going to force you into a corner. I'm not even going to ask you if you love me. Not tonight, anyway. But I do want to ask you something. Remember when I told you that I was guided to become a counselor? What do you think I meant by that?"

"I suppose you heard some kind of inner voice—maybe the voice of God."

"The inner voice *is* God. Sometimes it sounds as if the voice is coming from somewhere outside you, but it's just the echo of your inner voice. Everyone has God inside them. That includes you. It's time you started listening."

‡

Now that I was no longer in front of a class, I had lost control of my life. In this world where I was just another aging, single man I did not get to determine the curriculum. Everyone had their own curriculum, and the only way for me to keep my head above water was either to master all those curricula or to establish my own. But even if I could master those curricula, I didn't get to make up the essay questions or set the exams. My experience with Violet was proof enough of that—I could suggest the assignment, but it was out of my control as soon as it left my hands. Having lost my students, I had lost myself. Everything that had happened to me in the past several days was telling me that over and over again. I had convinced myself that I wanted to return to my youth, to reclaim possibility, to have a do-over, and here I was, as subject to the world as I was when I was five years old, except that when I was five I was still bathed in innocence, whereas now, I was burdened with experience. Innocence said, "Here is a pomegranate," and my five-year-old self took that imperfect globe, broke it open, and wondered at all the shiny, red kernels chambered inside it, crunching and tasting each one as if it were a world unto itself. Experience said, "Here is a pomegranate," and my sixty-year-old self, knowing what pomegranates were, considered only the messiness of cutting it open, staining my hands and sometimes my clothes with the indelible red juice, and the labour-intensive activity of trying to pry the seeds out, fretting all the while that the reward was not equal to the effort to obtain it.

Violet would look at me, holding the pomegranate in my hand like a golden apple of the Hesperides, and say, "Eat it and live forever." Deborah would look at me, holding the pomegranate in my hand like a woman's breast, and say, "It's what you've always wanted, full of beautiful red nipples." Esther would look at me, holding the pomegranate in my hand like a grenade with the pin in it, and say, "Time to make a decision." Angela would look at me, holding the pomegranate in my hand as if I expected it to be something else, and say, "Sometimes a pomegranate is just a pomegranate."

What is a cup of perked coffee, I wonder? Or a porch? Or a river? When one wonders a question, where does it go? Does it escape the wondering mind like smoke up a chimney to disappear into the vast atmosphere of the planet? Is there some layer of the stratosphere where they run out of propellant and drift about, tangling themselves with prayers that didn't have enough spiritual propulsion to make it to the ears of God? Perhaps the young years of all aging humans are stranded up there as well. Is there a telescopic lens that can find all these questions and prayers and lost years? I sit on my porch in the late evening, cup of coffee in hand, eyes aimed at the star-pricked sky, wondering. Perhaps the stars are those questions and prayers and lost years. Perhaps all the astronomers are looking through the wrong kinds of telescopes and that's why they haven't yet made this discovery. Perhaps I'm the only one who knows this. Whom should I tell?

Part Nine

Darest thou now O soul,
Walk out with me toward the unknown region,
Where neither ground is for the feet nor any path to follow?
                                               —*Walt Whitman*

"Makes sense to me."

I retrieved my eyes from the sky to focus on the body beside me from whence the voice came. Mr. Brautigan and I were stretched out on the hood of a derelict 1956 Ford Crown Victoria, leaning against the windshield, staring up at the night sky.

"You can see everything that's worth seeing from here," he said, tilting a bottle to his lips. He reached it over to me, without bringing his eyes down from the sky. "That group of stars up there," he said, pointing with his free hand up into the darkness, "those are the years of my lost youth, up until I was twelve years old. Sometimes they're hard to find—you have to be looking in exactly the right place, but you can only see them from here on the hood of this car. Strange how that is, but then life is a strange place to be."

I took a swig from the bottle. It was some kind of whiskey.
"Where is this?"
"This is Montana. I had some good times here."
"Do you miss this?"
"You can put it on the list."

I passed the bottle back to him. He took a long, slow swig. There was a kind of practiced beauty about the way he tilted his head back to match the tilt of his arm. If this were an Olympic event, he would have received tens across the board.

"You should have taught my novels. Why didn't you teach my novels?"

"I liked them too much."

"You taught *Franny and Zooey*. You seemed to like that pretty much."

"I thought my students could find their way around *Franny and Zooey* without leaving me behind. I think if I tried to teach *Trout Fishing in America* or *In Watermelon Sugar* I would have left myself behind, and you don't want to do that in front of a class."

"I taught a few courses."

"Yeah, but they were Creative Writing courses. That's different."

"I put myself on the line."

"You know what my favourite novel of yours is? *So The Wind Won't Blow It All Away*. Your last one."

"There was *An Unfortunate Woman*."

"I meant your last one that got published while you were still alive. But even so, it was the novel you wrote because you knew you were going to die soon."

"I just didn't know how, yet."

"I could tell it was your last novel because you looked at your twelve-year-old self as the best of all your selves, and he was gone forever. I get that."

"Well, I did leave you the gun."

"You knew exactly when your childhood ended—February 17, 1948, when you accidentally shot your best friend."

"I accidentally shot my childhood dead."

He passed the bottle back to me.

"How many people," he asked, "do you think still read that book?"

"Not enough. I've read it enough times to make up for a lot of those people who have never read it."

"You should have taught that book. Taken the risk. You still could."

"I retired."

"You can't retire from what you love doing. That's dying."

"Sometimes you just run out of gas."

"You can only run out of gas once. There are no filling stations. I know. I looked for them long enough."

I passed the bottle back to him. There was only one good swig left in it.

"You think my tank might not be empty, then?" I asked him.

"Drop a stone in it and see if it rattles around on the bottom."

"Do you feel that you got left behind by the world?"

"Maybe. It doesn't much matter now."

"Are you my guide?"

He slid down off the hood of the car and threw the empty bottle into the darkness. It flew off the arc of his arm with that same beauty of motion as when he was swigging its contents into his dream-ravaged body. I wanted to give him more things to throw into the darkness, just so I could watch him.

"For your sake, I hope not."

The darkness was a magnet pulling him away from the derelict car. He stumbled towards it because there was nothing else he could do. And then he just disappeared. I slid down off the hood of the car and took a few steps back from it to get as good a look at it as I could in the darkness. It was a classic two-tone—the bottom half and the roof a dark colour, maybe red, with the upper half, including the hood and trunk, white. I looked in the direction the car had come from and the direction in which it was pointed, but there was no road evident. There was the faint outline of a fence off to the right of the car, but I couldn't see what was being fenced in or out. I pulled open the driver's side door, which groaned in half-hearted resistance, and got in. Bench seats. Why did they ever get rid of those? Maybe there were just too comfortable. Big round steering wheel. Why did they get rid of those, too? When you had to turn a corner, you felt as if you were really making a graceful change of direction. I checked to see if there was a key in the ignition. There was. I turned it. Nothing. So, I just relaxed on that big, wide bench seat, my left hand on the steering wheel, my right arm stretched along the top of the seat, and pretended I was one of those cool guys that I never was.

‡

"The ingenious spirit of the American individual," said Mr. Whitman, sitting on the far side of the front seat beside me, passing his hand lightly across the dashboard. "Where are we going?"

"It doesn't work anymore."

"Too bad. Maybe we should get out and walk."

The dull thud of the doors closing seemed to trigger a shift in the sky and the geography. The darkness gave way in quick slow motion to a sunrise, and we were walking along a beach.

"I grew up here," he said, pausing to lean with both hands on his cane, staring out across the water. "Paumanok," he added, as if greeting an old friend. "Memory is a powerful force. Sometimes I like to lie in the sand and let it wash over me. I'm sure there are worse places to drown."

The sound of the ocean surf was the sound of time that had no beginning and no end.

"Down that way," he said, lifting his cane and pointing it down the coast, "are several sandbars, many over two hundred rods out from the shore. But here, here there's nothing to get in the way of the ocean's desire to court the shoreline. A rough courting it is, now and then. Many a ship has been wrecked along these shores, even with the lighthouses strung along the coast. Sometimes you can see exactly where it is you want to get to, you can be close enough that if you shouted to those waiting, they could hear you, but fate gets in between where you are and where you want to be and there's not much you can do about it.

"'O, Death! a black and pierceless pall
Hangs round thee, and the future state;
No eye may see, no mind may grasp
That mystery of fate.'"

"Those lines yours?"

"Mine."

"But they rhyme."

"I was just getting started. Hadn't yet left the European influence behind. In the winters," he continued, changing direction, "the south bay was shallow enough to freeze over, and we boys would go out onto the ice and break holes in it to catch eels. In the summers we would go clam digging; sometimes we'd gather seagull eggs. I sailed a boat on these waters, I walked these shores and inland and across to the other shore. I learned this island; I learned my self here. *Leaves of Grass* was born here and then I just let it grow up and get old, like me. But a man never stops being a boy."

I could remember being a boy, but I did stop being one.

"You get to the point," I said, "when memories overtake where you are and where you're going. I suppose it happens at different times for different people. It's happening to me now."

"How does it feel?"

"It feels as if there's nothing else I could possibly feel."

"Have you danced this world to the end of the song?"

"This world," I repeated.

The two words weighed more than a man my age could lift.

"*Leaves of Grass*—that was my world. Once I entered it I couldn't rightfully leave it without having to come back. Every time I came back—and I came back seven times—I brought something new with me, but I also changed what was already there. You can do that, you know. There are millions of suns left."

"It feels as if there's only one sun, and it's going down."

"Look in a different direction."

"Are you my guide?"

"No, she is."

I turned my eyes from the ocean and looked inland, towards where Mr. Whitman nodded his head. Paumonok—Long Island—gave way to a sloping, heather-covered moor. She seemed to rise out of the heather, her long, slim body swaying towards me; a large, brown-black dog at her side. Some way before she reached me, she leaned down and plucked a sprig of heather, which, when she finally reached me, she held out to me as a kind of greeting.

> "When days of Beauty deck the earth
> Or stormy nights descend,

How well my spirit knows the path
On which it aught to wend."

"'It seeks the consecrated spot,'" I continued,

"'Beloved in childhood years,
The space between is all forgot
Its sufferings and its tears.'

"My mother read that to me as a child. Emily?"
"Yes."

I turned back to Mr. Whitman to see if I could get a further understanding of what had just happened. There was no Mr. Whitman, no shoreline, no ocean. Just moor. I turned back to examine the young woman who stood before me. She was as tall as I was, but seemed taller because of the narrowness of her body and of her face, which was framed by parallel hanging waves of brown hair, and by her dress, which hung without interruption from her shoulders to her feet. The colour of her eyes shifted from slate blue to grey to hazel, depending on the extent to which I let the heather—which billowed out all around us, giving way in this direction and that to barer ground, and a sprig of which I now held in my hand—supply the foreground in which she stood.

"You may walk with me if you wish," she said, looking at my feet rather than at my face.

She did not wait for my answer, but walked past me so that I had to turn to follow her. We followed no path that I could see, though it seemed clear that she had walked this way many times. Now and then she would pause to lean down and pick a spray of bilberry or a feather left behind by some bird I did not recognize, though from her smile as she held it up to the sun, it was clear that she did. We did not speak for the better part of the hour that we walked, until we came to a series of springs in the midst of grass, whose shade of green I had never before seen. We were soon presented with a stepped waterfall, a few feet in height.

"The Meeting of the Waters," she said, choosing a large stone to sit on and rest. "Some days, when the wind cannot decide which direction to come from, I can follow this stream and find myself by the marsh where you grew up. That is how I first saw you. You were riding a hobby-horse down a hill. We were watching you. All of us."

"Why are you here now?"

"I have always been here," she said, looking around her as if defining the space around us with her eyes.

"Okay, why I am here with you?"

"For the storm."

"What storm?"

"Be patient. It's coming. Can't you feel how the air is changing?"

She said this with an air of excitement, that kind of excitement that only a child feels. Watching her entire aspect vibrate with anticipation, I could recall that energy in myself, realizing at the same time that it was something I had not experienced in decades. And now I *could* feel it; I could physically sense the air changing. Emily took my hand and led me to a bower formed by large, overhanging trees. She crouched down, her body tensed and yet, at the same time, opened to the possibility of what was about to happen. A sudden gust of wind shouted the branches of the trees under which we were waiting, the sky darkened to the thickest shade of grey before it must be called black, and the first heavy drops of rain spattered the leaves above us and the ground in front of us like a drum tattoo calling us home. A burst of thunder exploded overhead; we almost expected to see the sky painted with the thousand sparks of fireworks. Instead, fractured lines of lightning veined the sky. The drumming of the rain quickened into a loud, uninterrupted shush in the midst of which Emily's voice escaped her—the sound a child makes when she is presented with a new toy. Her hand, still holding mine, squeezed its life, like a palpable exhalation, into my fingers, consequently inhaling my life into hers.

There are many ways to describe the shiver of love. Sometimes it clutches at your stomach, as if that organ were to suddenly become weightless inside your weighted body. Sometimes your arms are pulled into your body as if to keep something inside that must not escape lest your vital energy be dissipated. Sometimes it is a catching of the breath that vibrates the length of your body, from your chest down into your feet. That is the shiver. The love has its own complex set of definitions. The love that shivered Emily, and me as part of its echo, in that moment was not anchored by any kind of lust, nor by any of the typical kinds of desire that one human feels for another, for we were not merely human in that moment. We were creations of the storm, as the storm was a creation of some mystical urge in our own spirits. As always, such experiences are beyond the capacity of words, as they must be in order to be truly profound. Even as I was in the midst of that mystery, I knew I had not experienced it before in my life and I knew that I could not experience it again. But experience is the wrong word altogether. The language of religion and of spirituality often opposes experience with revelation, the former being subject to conventional means of communication, in that it is something that has been or can be shared with others, the latter being something purely and perfectly personal and not transferable.

The Meeting of the Waters swelled into a torrent of supernal voices all having chosen to express themselves through the same element. I cannot calculate how long the storm took to exhaust itself; it was eternal while it lasted. At some indistinct point, the thunder surrendered to silence, the electricity of lightning was unplugged, and storm darkness was replaced with night darkness, as was evidenced by the speckling of the sky with stars, and all that shifted as indistinctly into the dawn, which blazed the eastern horizon with fiery pinks and oranges. Emily and I had not moved in all that time, and as we stood up, still hand in hand, we unfolded the past into the present, a place I did not easily recognize. When she let go of my hand, the heat of the now risen sun filled the space between us.

"Imagine," she said, as much to the rolling moor and the sky as to me.

‡

I felt as if I were being imagined. I felt as if the only way I could anchor myself to this world, whichever one it was that I was supposed to be in, was to ask some great and important question that only Emily could answer. I suppose she could read all that in my eyes as they travelled across the geography of her face, looking for somewhere to rest.

"I will speak for myself, but you will recognize your own self where you will. What matters in all our stories is not so much ourselves as the place in which we find ourselves. I could not find myself when I was at Cowan Bridge or Roe Head or Law Hill. I learned before my times in school, during those times, and after those times that I lived most essentially within myself, took all my inspiration from within myself, unless it was from nature, but nature was myself. And yet, I could not divorce myself from my surroundings, as unpleasant as some of them were. So, it was that I defended myself against a philosophically pernicious external environment, or at least justified myself within it, by constructing a language of the imagination, where all stories, including our own, truly live. This understanding can be learned, but it cannot be taught. It belongs to the innocence of youth and is necessarily mistreated by age."

She aimed her gaze at me, but only for a second or two, giving it back to the sky where it felt safer to penetrate.

"I may be your guide, but I am a reluctant one. My poems were meant for no one but me. I know how to let them roam wild, yet come to me when I call. When others call them, they do not always present themselves as who they are. You must write your own poems and live inside those. However, since your mother chose my poems as a place of connection between yourselves, I will give you one last poem of my own. But before I do that, there is one thing you can do for me."

"Ask it."

"Come, there is a stream winding through the copse down below."

The purple of heather below harmonized the blue of sky above, until the green of trees and the silver of water replaced them. We walked along the bank of the stream.

"There," she said, pointing ahead.

'There' consisted of an opening, at the far end of which seemed to be a stand of bulrushes. As we got closer to them, the geography began to shapeshift, until, on reaching the bulrushes I looked to my left to see the rise of Garter Snake Hill. She walked around the edge of the bulrushes and up the slope of the hill. I followed her to the top, where we sat on a fallen log and looked out across the marsh to our right and the lake in front of us.

"In my second novel I tell the story of a young woman who teaches at a hedge school situated in a wood between the three villages of Gravenskirk, Mallows End, and High Graydon. The young woman comes from somewhere between Liverpool and Blackpool and is Heathcliff's younger sister. Neither she nor Heathcliff is aware that the one has a brother and the other a sister. Being the sister of Heathcliff, meaning that her parentage is questionable, she had a similarly difficult life as a child and learned to defend herself against those who would take advantage of her. She punched and kicked at anyone who would dare to confine her spirit in ways that she found repugnant to her sense of herself. Eventually, to protect herself, she took to dressing as a boy and later as a man, all the while making her way in the most dangerous parts of Liverpool. She formed no close relationships for fear of giving herself away. But she had curiosity and imagination, the both of which nurtured her when nothing else was made available to her. She borrowed books when she could and stole them if she could not borrow them. She becomes a very learned person, but finds that the development of her philosophic view of the world now separates her from it, as much as did her rude upbringing in her beginning years. In time, she meets a young man with whom she falls in love, but she is unable to reveal herself."

Here, Emily paused to study some of the fallen leaves around the log on which we were sitting. I wondered if she were recalling someone she might have loved, someone who has remained forever unknown to all those who have studied her life and her writing.

"What is her name?"

"Her name is Alexandra. His name is Alexander."

"What happens to her?"

Emily rose from the log and began to walk down the slope towards the lake. At the shingle bar, which separated the marsh from the lake, she leaned down and picked up one of the large, flat stones.

"I've never seen such stones."

"They're good for skipping."

"Skipping?"

I took the stone from her hand and skipped it across the surface of the lake. For the first time, I heard her laugh. It was closer to a giggle than a laugh.

"Do that again," she pleaded.

I skipped another stone. The same giggle.

"Show me how."

I picked a stone to suit the size of her hand. I stood behind her, cupping her right hand in mine.

"The other hand," she said placing the stone in her left hand.

"I don't know if I can do this, other way around."

"You're a teacher, are you not?"

Still standing behind her, I cupped her left hand in mine, placing my right hand on her right shoulder so as to guide her in the proper swing of her upper body. My face pressed lightly against the back of her head. Her hair smelled of sunlight and autumn.

"Is this necessary?"

She leaned slightly forward, away from me. I could see the blush on her cheek.

"I'm sorry."

"But if it is necessary," she said, staring towards the water and leaning back towards me.

"It's mostly in how you hold the stone in your hand. Like this," I said, taking the stone and holding it, index finger curved around the edge of the stone.

It took several tries, but eventually she managed to get a single skip. Having succeeded, she sat down on the shingle, wrapping her arms around her knees, pulling them up towards her chin. She stared out across the lake, commanding all the world around her to be none other than it was.

"What is the thing you wanted me to do for you?"

"You have done it. Now, lie back on these warm stones and I will give you my poem."

I stretched myself across my uncomfortable bed, loosening my resistance until I could imagine myself lying in a field of heather. I closed my eyes.

"Often rebuked, yet always back returning
    To those first feelings that were born with me,
And leaving busy chase of wealth and learning
    For idle dreams of things which cannot be:

Today, I will seek not the shadowy region;
    Its unsustaining vastness waxes drear;
And visions rising, legion after legion,
    Bring the unreal world too strangely near.

I'll walk, but not in old heroic traces,
    And not in paths of high morality,
And not among the half-distinguished faces,
    The clouded forms of long-past history.

I'll walk where my own nature would be leading:
    It vexes me to choose another guide:
Where the grey flocks in ferny glens are feeding;
    Where the wild wind blows on the mountain side.

What have those lonely mountains worth revealing?
    More glory and more grief than I can tell:
The earth that wakes *one* human heart to feeling
    Can centre both the worlds of Heaven and Hell."

The sun burned softly through my eyelids, dancing flecks of orange light against a red background.

"I'm glad you got to hear the rest of that poem."

It was my mother's voice.

"No, don't open your eyes. There are places you can see from behind your eyelids that can't be seen any other way. That's why I read the poems to you when you were drifting away from the daytime world."

She pressed her fingers ever so lightly against my eyelids. The pattern of orange flecks shifted into different choreographies.

"See how easy it is to change the world. You are no longer rebuked. You are returning."

‡

The shingle bar, with me lying on its stony deck, was a ship floating on water that barely had any waves pulsing it. The sun, still burning through the thin flesh of my eyelids, got only slightly closer then only slightly farther away because of the barely waves. Sometimes, this is what it takes to shift a man from one world towards another—just lying on the stony deck of his childhood, feeling each single stone pressing into his body like acupuncture needles on the appropriate meridians. Sometimes, when a man does this, he knows when to open his eyes and look up at the sky. He knows when to stand up and start walking across the shingle, which is now just shingle, back towards Garter Snake Hill (everyone has a Garter Snake Hill), back along the creek that could quench every spiritual thirst, even when you didn't know you were thirsty. Back into the past that is always present. In all the geography classes I took in school, I could never find any maps that had the present clearly marked on them. For example, the desk I was imprisoned at, surrounded by other desks with other inmates my age, all of us wishing we could be anywhere else in the world, or any other world—that desk was never on those maps.

I walked the creek backwards through my own ten thousand footsteps, first emerging from the bulrushes to witness the last class I taught. I walked into the classroom for the last time, letting the awareness of finality descend upon me like beautiful fat flakes of snow through the fuzzy halo of a streetlamp on a rarely travelled road. I stood there in silence at the front of the class for a minute or so, the snow falling peacefully, making everything peaceful. None of my students knew this was my last class, so I broke the silence with that simple statement: "This is my last class." Then I let the snow keep falling for a bit longer.

"'What we call the beginning is often the end,'" I began, reciting the opening lines from the last section of the fourth of Eliot's *Four Quartets*. I recited the whole section by heart, from heart. "'The end is where we start from'"—could they possibly understand what Eliot meant, what I meant for myself in saying those words? I wasn't sure I understood it as fully as I hoped I would. I knew this was an end, but I didn't really know what I was starting.

"'Every phrase and every sentence is an end and a beginning.'" How many phrases and sentences had I written, had I read, in all my years as a student and as a teacher? Ending and beginning—I knew intellectually that this was happening for me, to me, but I couldn't yet feel it anywhere else in my body or in my soul. What had become of my soul?

> "'We shall not cease from exploration
> And the end of all our exploring
> Will be to arrive where we started
> And know the place for the first time.'"

I scanned the pairs of eyes staring back at me, trying, hoping to find some sort of recognition. *Can you see me?* I shouted at them from the silence of my mind. *Can you hear me?* I knew better than to ask it out loud. I used to be their age; I used to be indifferent and confused and hopeful and angry just like them.

> "'At the source of the longest river
> The voice of the hidden waterfall
> And the children in the apple-tree
> Not known, because not looked for
> But heard, half-heard, in the stillness
> Between two waves of the sea.'

Do you understand, I wanted to ask them out loud, *that you are caught between two waves of the sea? Do you have a boat? Do you know how to swim?* I paused and let the stillness and the beautiful fat flakes of snow keep falling. I looked to see if any of my students were looking at those flakes, if any of them would hold out their tongues to catch the whiteness.

> "'Quick now, here, now, always—
> A condition of complete simplicity
> (Costing not less than everything)'"

I paused again. I repeated the last two lines.

> "'And all shall be well and
> All manner of thing shall be well.'"

I waited to hear someone, any one of them, ask, "Will it?" No one did. I smiled at them—what kind of smile was it? A smile of recognition? Of resignation? Of acceptance? Of good-bye? I left the room, walking slowly enough so as not to disturb the easy rhythm, the eternally patient patterns of falling snow.

I continued down the creek, pausing at the bend where I came upon the realization, five years ago, that my teaching days were numbered. That was the place where, standing in front of a classroom full of first-year literature students, I knew that what I needed to teach them, what they needed to learn from me, could only happen on a subliminal level, the level below the hard, structured surface of the curriculum, the level where, for a moment that seems to last forever, we all fear we are going to drown because there is no land to crawl up on, only ocean where we must surrender ourselves to absence of rigidity—rigidity of process, of spirit, of intention. Or we were all floating helplessly in space, having gone for a spacewalk and forgotten to attach ourselves to the lifeline. Whatever required texts that were on the course outline needed to be treated as space junk careening towards us, and there was no telling if it would smash us to pieces. Or . . . there were several metaphors to describe the situation. I used them all out loud to my classroom full of impressionable students, realizing all the while that my very words were the space junk they hoped wouldn't smash through the still developing membrane of their identity. There were, though, the few precious Violets scattered here and there looking for roots in that cluttered and boundless space.

Further along the creek towards the bridge at Meadow Wood Road, I sat down on the crumbling shale bank and stared at the water rippling through the semester when I tried to apply the method of grading that Robert Pirsig described when he taught English at a college in Bozeman, Montana. I had come late to *Zen and the Art of Motorcycle Maintenance*, in the same way that I came late to most of the important things in my life. He decided not to give grades to his students until the semester was over. He would keep track of the grades himself, but the students would not know what grade they received for any of their assignments. They could no longer be propelled forward by the need to improve or maintain their grades; the only method of propulsion left them was their own interest, their own intellectual barometers. I don't know how he got away with doing that, especially in the 1950s American education system, but several of my students went to the Department Chair immediately after I returned their first assignments without any grades on them. The Department Chair, fearing disruption of any kind, sided with the students' fear and demanded that I cease my experiment. I retreated, and spent the rest of my teaching years trying to suppress my disappointment in my department for lacking what Pirsig called "gumption," and in myself for surrendering without a fight.

I got up and continued walking, the path before me sometimes apparent only in that it followed the course of the creek. There were low-hanging tree branches, reaching out across the creek, that I had to duck under, almost crawl under, or detour around, finding myself temporarily stumbling through those parts of the woods that seemed to consciously resist the intrusion of human movement. In one such place I leaned back into the thickness of unfettered green growth and was held up as if I had sat myself down in a lazyboy chair. Here, I watched myself on the edge of tenure, teaching a class in which two of my tenured colleagues sat near the back to observe my teaching skills and report back to the committee to discuss whether or not I should, indeed, be offered tenure. Such processes were formalities, at best, given that one's publication record was the strongest determinant of qualification.

I never liked publishing academic articles. The only people who ever read them were other professors looking for material to quote in their own articles or books, or graduate students who had to learn what every other academic thought about a given subject before they dared to express their own points of view, which, by the time they slogged through all the material, were too often stillborn. And on and on the intellectual incest would go. I hated publishing. I hated having to teach a class in which two of my tenured colleagues sat like Cherubim with their blazing swords they really didn't know how to use because they didn't really know what the gates they were guarding were for. I chose to teach something by Whitman because I knew him well and because I had done my first, unsuccessful doctoral dissertation on him and Richard Brautigan, and I wanted to show the Cherubim the continuity and development of my thought, knowing full well that they could not possibly have read that failed dissertation. I chose the poem "O Living Always, Always Dying":

> O living always, always dying!
> O the burials of me past and present,
> O me while I stride ahead, material, visible, imperious as ever;
> O me, what I was for years, now dead (I lament not, I am content;)
> O to disengage myself from those corpses of me, which I turn and look at where I cast them,
> To pass on, (O living! always living!) and leave the corpses behind.

Would the Cherubim get the reference to Deucalion throwing the bones of his mother over his shoulder to repopulate the earth? Would they get the irony? Probably not. Could they possibly understand how utterly personal the poem was for me? Definitely not. One gathers small joys where one can. But I did get tenure—a bonus prize.

I made my way back to the creek. There was the place, just where the creek split into two before joining itself together again, where I taught my very first class when I was a doctoral student. It was a first-year course in introductory literature. It was my job to introduce my students to the study of literature—this was well before I understood that my real job was to introduce them to a study of themselves through literature. I had to cover the four major genres: poetry, plays, short stories, and novels. What order I did these in was up to me. That very first class, though, was also me introducing myself to my students and them to me.

"Are you a real professor?"

This from a consciously sassy blonde-haired girl/woman in the front row. I could tell she was one of those self-appointed instigators of disequilibrium who ruled her high school classes because she needed to challenge those who were supposed to challenge her but didn't or couldn't.

"I'm a PhD student."

"Why don't we get a real professor?"

She didn't care what the answers to her questions were; she hardly cared about the questions themselves. She just wanted to be engaged.

"Why don't you take that chip off your shoulder, set it down, relax, and reserve your judgment until at least the end of this class?"

She smiled, still full of sass, but somewhat pleased, I assumed, to have met a worthy opponent, at least for a few minutes.

"Karma Repair Kit: Items 1-4."

I had decided to begin with poetry. With Richard Brautigan.

"1. Get enough food to eat,
and eat it.

2. Find a place to sleep where it is quiet,
     and sleep there.
  3. Reduce intellectual and emotional noise
     until you arrive at the silence of yourself,
     and listen to it.
  4.   "

That's the poem I wished I'd begun with. I would have let the absence of number 4 hang in the air like a bomb or a parachute about to fall on their heads. If I had that moment to do over again, that's how I would have begun. I would have challenged the shit out of them, especially of the blonde instigator. As it was, my teaching testicles had not yet dropped, and I began with Andrew Marvell's "To His Coy Mistress." A big mistake. They had been *Carpe Diem*ed into submission in high school. They wanted something else, anything else, to seize on to other than that poem. I should have checked that. I eventually managed to recover, to the point where my course evaluations at the end of the semester were around seventy percent. The blonde instigator never showed up again after the first class.

I walked on past the small island in the creek, back to where the two watery veins had yet to separate. The bridge wasn't far away now. So far, I had recognized all the stops along the way, but I didn't expect to see Mr. Sullivan, my grade eight teacher, sitting on a weather-beaten wooden chair in the middle of the creek. His pant legs were rolled up, his bare feet planted in the water. He was pointed downstream. When you're twelve years old, you don't expect to see your teacher anywhere except in the classroom. Even to see him in the village buying a newspaper or a quart of milk would have seemed extraordinary. But sitting in the middle of the creek?

"The view's much better from here," he said. "Surely, you stood in the middle of this creek when you were a boy. Come here and sit by me," he motioned with his hand to the empty chair beside him.

I took off my shoes and socks, rolled up my pant legs, walked to the chair, and sat down beside him.

"Feels good, the water running through your toes, don't you think? Almost as if it's running out of your toes; as if you're feeding the creek. You remember that feeling? I'd forgotten it. You're a lucky man to have grown up in such a place," he said, his eyes doing a slow scan of the immediate horizon.

We sat in silence for a few minutes. I had no idea what to say to him, or if I was even supposed to say anything at all.

"Did I teach you well?" he asked. "I hope I did. I tried my best. You were a good student; you didn't really need much teaching, at least as far as 'book learning' was concerned. But you were a timid boy. I could tell you were afraid of the world and it was all you could do to keep that fear down. Was I wrong?"

He was my teacher for grades six, seven, and eight; I had never considered the possibility that he might be wrong about anything. Why would he ask a twelve-year-old boy such a question?

"I suppose you've figured out how hard it is to be a teacher. It's the greatest responsibility there is. More so for me because I taught children at such a young and impressionable age. All of you were caught between having forgotten your identity when you were five years old and figuring out that you either had to rediscover it or forge a new one. Of course, none of you were conscious of the fact that that was what was going on. It was an enormous responsibility I had. You taught them as young adults who believed they had discovered who they were or who were still so lost that they might never find themselves. That's a big responsibility, too. Did it keep you awake at nights? It did me. Cold sweats sometimes. I kept a bottle of whiskey in my drawer, and every afternoon when I got home from school, I'd take it out and dare it to dare me. I lived alone, you know, in that small apartment above a barbershop. Came all the way out here from the east coast. All kinds of reasons for that, but you don't need to know them. It was a lonely job, being a teacher. And, of course, I was the principal, too. Did I teach you well? Did I help you to navigate your life?"

"I don't know that anyone could have helped me. But you didn't harm me."

"I guess that's something."

We slipped back into silence. The gurgle of the creek took up all the sonic space there was.

"You did fine," I said. "I liked you."

"Did you ever stay in touch with Dana, the pretty young red-headed girl that sat the next row over and a couple of seats down? She was as sweet on you as a girl could be."

I had not thought of Dana in decades, but as soon as Mr. Sullivan mentioned her name, I could see her twelve-year-old face before me. She was shy and smart, and I had no idea she liked me. Would it have made any difference if I did?

"She liked me?"

"I guess that's my answer. Too bad you lost touch with her. I could tell she was the kind of girl that would have stayed true to you forever if you had recognized the beauty she had to offer you—and I don't just mean how pretty she was. She was an old soul. You missed something special there."

Add her to the list, I thought. And then I thought, *If you wanted to be a good teacher, you should have taught me about Dana. You could have changed my life. Isn't that what good teachers are supposed to do?* But whom was I kidding? I wouldn't have known how to respond to her. Hell, if I met her now, I still wouldn't know how to respond to her.

"I should have sat in this creek when I was your teacher," Mr. Sullivan said, more to himself than to me. "I could have learned—remembered—a thing or two. That's the thing about teaching—you always wish you could do it over again, better. That's what we retired teachers do—we wish backwards in time where we used to march forwards in time. Do you remember that book report you did on Peggy's Cove? You'd never been there—I don't know why it was you chose that little book—you didn't know that I grew up not far from there on the coast of Nova Scotia. What I remember most about that book report was your fascination with who Peggy was. You didn't like the idea that Peggy was probably short for Margaret and that Champlain had named the bay Saint Margaret's Bay after his mother. You preferred the story that young Peggy was the only survivor of a shipwreck near the bay. The book report was supposed to be an exercise in how to summarize a piece of writing, but you spun a whole story about Peggy, about how she was a young girl coming over from England with her family, and when she was shipwrecked she wandered the bay for months before anyone knew she had survived. According to you, she was a fearless young girl who, as she grew older, was courted by every young man for miles around, but she refused every offer. She grew old, but remained as beautiful as she had always been—oh yes, you were careful to emphasize that fact about her beauty—and people would come to her to seek advice in times of trouble. I still can't figure out how you didn't understand about Dana."

I had forgotten about that book report. I could recall vague details, but I didn't remember telling my own story instead of summarizing the one that was in the book.

"If I sit here long enough in this creek," I said to Mr. Sullivan, "do you think that Dana or Peggy would eventually come walking by?"

"Oh, yes. You're not the first person to come walking by since I've been sitting here."

"How long have you been here?"

"Long enough and not long enough. I miss it, you know, the teaching."

That was his truth. That was his beauty. I stood up and put my hand on his shoulder. He reached his hand across his body and put it on my hand. There was nothing more that could be said. I sloshed my feet through the water back towards the bank. I stuffed my socks in my shoes, tied their laces together, hung them around my neck, and stepped back into the creek, continuing my way towards the bridge.

Just around the final bend I arrived at my first day of school when I was five years old. Intimations of immortality, indeed. I was like Isaac, about to be sacrificed to some god, but there was no one to stay Abraham's hand, and there passed away a glory from the earth. I don't remember the exact moment when the knife sliced into my heart. Maybe there wasn't an exact moment; maybe it was the proverbial death by a thousand cuts, by eight grades of elementary school and five years of high school, at which point I took myself off to university, having learned to hold the knife and keep stabbing myself with it.

> "Thou little Child, yet glorious in the might
> Of heaven-born freedom on thy being's height,
> Why with such earnest pains dost thou provoke
> The years to bring the inevitable yoke
> Thus blindly with thy blessedness at strife?"

I stepped out of the water and climbed the low bank to the path, the bridge now looming in front of me. As I approached the bridge I looked along the road and saw a young boy speeding down the hill on his bike. There was a purple and grey metal lunch box in the front carrier attached to the handlebars; a small leather satchel with its strap hanging over the edge of the carrier. He was on his way to school. As he came level with the bridge, coasting at full speed, I noticed them, all of them, standing all around me. The leaves were full of children. One of them called out.

"Hey, Levi! Wait up!"

He slammed his heels backwards on his pedals, the bike skidding to a stop. He steered his bike towards the young girl who was standing off to my right. All the others had disappeared.

☦

> *Is there anything more beautiful*
> *than the bow of a ship*
> *touching the new world?*
>   —*Richard Brautigan*

Acknowledgements

I must begin by thanking my oldest and best friend, Steve, for the opening line of the novel, which he thought was just part of a conversation we had about relationships. It was at Peter and Margo's farmhouse somewhere around 1971 that I was introduced to Richard Brautigan and J.D. Salinger. Thanks, also, to the inspiring genius of Walt Whitman, Emily Brontë, T.S. Eliot, Sylvia Plath, Olive Higgins Prouty, and whoever really did write First Corinthians. Thanks to Sheila Pandora Rose for listening to me read this whole novel out loud—twice—and offering her honest and sympathetic feedback. Finally, but perhaps most importantly, I want to thank two people, in particular: Johanna Bates, who read my first novel (which still awaits a publisher) many years ago and took me on as a client. She believed in me from the beginning and was tireless in her efforts to get me published, which she did with *A Stone in My Pocket*; and Anne Bougie-Johnson, who took over the reins from Johanna and has continued to faithfully shepherd me along this crazy path of being a writer. I owe these two women a debt of gratitude that is beyond the power of the words on this page.